C000212969

THE WAKING

THE WAKING

Matthew Smith

WUNDOR

Editions

First published in Great Britain in 2017 by Wundor Editions

Wundor Editions Ltd, 35B Fitzjohn's Avenue, London NW3 5JY

www.wundoreditions.com

Copyright © Matthew Smith 2017

Matthew Smith has asserted his right under the Copyright, Designs and
Patents Act 1988 to be identified as the author of this work

Book Design – Matthew Smith

ISBN 978-0-9956541-5-0

This book is sold subject to the condition that it shall not, by way of
trade or otherwise, be lent, resold, hired out, or otherwise circulated
without the publisher's prior consent in any form of binding or cover
other than that in which it is published and without a similar condition,
including this condition, being imposed on the subsequent purchaser

Printed and bound in Great Britain by TJ International Ltd

For Vix

The street turns in silence. I'm running up the white spiral staircase that leads to our front door. The handle burns. I pause on the threshold: a babble of voices drifts out into the lustre of the evening.

'If I pour it slowly, don't I look like the woman in the painting?'

'Which painting are you thinking of, darling?'

This could be any evening after school.

'I'm afraid the light's all wrong.'

'Can everyone be quiet? You're wrecking the mood.'

I drop my bag in the hall and turn, as always, to watch the trees sway through the door frame, try to finish the thoughts I have been following.

Open the next door onto the uproar.

'Please try to keep your arm still.'

'Surely the bowl will overflow!'

'Not if she does it properly!'

Now the scene is identifiable.

My brother stands with his camera aimed at my sister, who slowly tips a jug of milk into a bowl, forehead troubled with concentration. My mother and father sit at a safe distance, a chorus of approval and apprehension. Jonny is pretending not to enjoy himself, breaking his focus as I enter to bewail the lack of seriousness invested in the exercise.

The light moves closer to horizontal, floods the room, making Jenny's hair a cataract of gold that falls from her shoulder to soak in the milk.

She giggles.

'My hair's in the milk!'

Laughter rising.

'My hair's in the damn milk!'

'Jenny!' Mum says tersely.

Uncontrollable laughter.

'My hair's in the goddamn milk!'

Jonny stops trying not to laugh.

'Flick it back!'

'Ignore that instruction!' Dad rumbles.

Too late. The French windows are constellated with beads of white as the room disappears in the camera flash.

'I got it!' Jonny cries.

My mother looks at me, embarrassed at having been caught laughing with her hand over her mouth, and I wonder now how many times she might have sat amongst us, enchanted beneath her usual mask of indifference.

This is how my mother comes to mind: just out of reach, or falling to a great distance away from me. She died fifteen years ago, when I was ten.

Often when I picture her, I see her move from a place of solitude into a dark room. A beam of light slips from the door ajar behind her. Sometimes the room is lit, and a dress she wore through my early childhood floods the space with colour. A deep-water perfume unfolds, redolent of low cloud, and I scan slowly up to her face, which may or may not emerge from the quickening vapours.

Then a stairwell opens up. She seems to be looking for an exit, which I will dutifully provide.

Isabel, the middle-child.

The spiral staircase was Mum's idea.

'Interested in spirals,' said Dad, 'like all serious writers.'

I had imagined a thin, delicate structure stretching up to a door on the roof. It only reached the front entrance, but the clearance of the stone steps was controversial enough in our part of Hampstead.

'Do these people like spirals because they are pretty?' I asked.

Dad thought about this.

'Yes. Among other reasons.'

'Because you can slide down them.'

'Can you? They're certainly difficult to climb.'

I was too young to question the necessity of the staircase at the time, but I remember listening at a door one day, hearing an old friend of my mother's telling her that it had to go. It had become a symbol of a widely perceived 'craziness'. Her friend was ushered quickly down said staircase. One shrug, eyes widening, from Mum and the neighbourhood vaporised. However, she maintained that friends must be heard out, and if forced to confess, she would admit that she cared what they thought. We never saw that one again.

As you know, my mother was the acclaimed novelist, Marianne Sykes. Her first two books still sell well. The third has its proponents on the wilder shores of academia.

It was around this time, when I was nine, that she began her final book, never to be completed.

Her first work is the literary novel that everyone reads. Naked Light draws on the walled, heavily aestheticized world of a heat-drenched French estate. The intimidating, neatly clipped topiary and pristine neoclassical statues of the place press themselves on the senses. The much-loved young heroine, Celine Curtis, visiting the home of her fiancé, is gradually suffocated by social and psychological forces that she does not understand.

It was a hit with the critics. John Fall wrote in the TLS: 'Not only has Sykes seen fit to install herself immediately in the upper reaches of English literature's starry firmament, but in doing so she has altered the lie of the sky slightly, constellations have shifted: as after the emergence of all great writers, what went before must now be seen differently.' Her second work widened the sensory flush of Naked Light. Her dedication to physical feeling reined in the dreamy journeys her characters made in their minds, constantly delivering them back to the moment. They were perpetually bemused by the deep intricacies of experience: time and its effects on the body, the cosmos spinning around puny minds, other people and their secrets. No other living writer matched her personal standards. Many critics found fault with Thunder, Lightning: 'a painted world', 'empty style' and 'brimming with ideas that are placed out of reach – like visiting an arcane museum in which everything glitters behind plate glass.' But the bad reviews contradicted one another enough to suggest that none of them hit the mark. Fall was best on the second book: 'A novel of colour and sunlight containing a fearsome darkness.'

The problems started, so my father would tell me later, with the publication of her third book, The Black Cloche. Here it was not just the quality of the work that was questioned – and widely so – but her own lucidity. The darker threads that had always run through her work thickened and tangled in its dense, chapterless mass. The treelined avenues and artists' studios of the earlier books gave way to shadowy rooms, dilating pupils. The infamous torture scenes were universally derided. The autograph hunters who knocked on the door now looked a little less fresh-faced. Her behaviour became more eccentric. I was told at school that my mother was weird, a judgement that points in retrospect to other, unseen mothers. The critics opened their phantasmal jaws.

Even her champion, John Fall, deserted her: 'It began well before its more chilling aspects overran the book.'

Mum was one of those writers for whom the vastness of their early success looks fit to carry them through a run of poorly received works and beyond. Unswervingly, she set about the follow-up to The Black Cloche, continuing along the path she had lain out for herself. But something in the forward flash of her destiny stammered like a fading neuron.

Let me correct that.

As a person she seemed to have sputtered to a halt, but as a writer she was producing her most mystifying work yet. It was as though half of her neural pathways had given themselves over to cope with twice the creative pressure. She was immovable, producing words, pages slowly like a bee compacting its hive from unseen fluff and oils. She worked in her study with a single lamp and the curtains drawn, like in the 'early days', she said. She only wore black. The work was never finished: Midnightsong.

'It's not a novel,' her publisher said, after reading the earliest pages.

I think it was the beginning of one. I have spent many months trying to understand this last, greatest work of Marianne Sykes – or rather, the part of it that she has left us.

I'd always imagined the onus would be on me to approach my mother, so to speak, to venture towards my memories of her. However, a stranger appeared at my flat a couple of years ago, and my mother began to approach me.

But I'll start with the story of her death.

The Earrings

I pushed the mirror firmly into the grass, backed off. It gleamed white at a distance. I approached it: a fallen piece of sky rippled in the green. I fell to my knees, darted forwards, added myself to the frame. I had anticipated a silhouette of my head and breeze-swept hair, but the mirror turned the sky's light up to my face and a soft glow slid across my skin. Then I was standing again.

I scanned the garden.

After a time, I heard voices at the front of the house. My parents saying goodbye to Jonny and Jenny.

Jonny appeared at the French windows and slipped outside. He came down the steps to the top of the garden and trotted towards me. Walked past me and leaned over the mirror.

'They've gone,' he said. 'What's the mirror for?'

I sat silent, examining the soles of my slip-ons.

'Where've they gone?' I said finally.

'To the party. You know that.'

'Which party?'

'Isabel.'

'The one at the end of the road?'

'Isabel! You know where they've gone.'

Jonny lay down on the grass and put his hands behind his head. 'What's the mirror for?'

I looked up at the sky, frowned at near-horizontal sunlight.

'Where's Jenny?' I said.

'She's indoors.'

'No one coming?'

'We're old enough now.'

He shook his head.

'When are they back?' I said.

'Shut up.'

'I don't have all the answers, Jonny.'

'You don't have any of them.'

'I really can't remember whether someone's coming.'

'How boring.'

'Who is?'

'All this time.'

'Oh.'

I held up my arms to look at the goose pimples forming under the soft hair.

'It's cold,' I said.

'Put a jumper on.'

'You just say what Dad says.' I pulled my hair out of my eyes. 'And anyway, I don't want to go back into the empty house.'

'Why not?'

'It'll be dark soon.'

'You don't make any sense.' He rolled over onto his stomach. 'Besides. Jenny's in there. And she's fine.'

He pulled up some bits of grass.

'Pretending all the time,' I said.

'Who's pretending?'

I turned to the house, a block of white that beamed against the brown brick of the terrace on either side. Jenny appeared at the far left window on the ground floor. Her face was expressionless, pressed against the glass. Jonny followed my gaze and waved at Jenny, mouthed 'Okay?'

Jenny didn't move.

'She looks like a ghost,' I said.

My sister slid suddenly below the window frame.

'Standing on a chair,' said Jonny. 'I've seen her do that. We should get her out to play.'

'She's okay.'

He nodded vaguely.

'What'll we do?' he said.

'Wait. See what happens.'

'That sounds like a boring game.'

'Something always happens. You just have to be patient.'

My mind was blank, pale grey like the total cloud you get hours before a thunderstorm. I was on my feet again, scanning the garden, tilting my head slowly from side to side.

Waiting.

Jonny shifted onto his knees.

'They have gone, you know,' he said. 'A hundred per cent.'

I turned round.

'I know.'

I grinned at Jonny. He grinned back.

'So what's this mirror for?' he said.

'Oh, that. A game. It was on TV.'

I went to the nearest bush, produced an empty wine bottle. He frowned.

'I think you need a magnifying glass for that,' he said.

'No! It's called... I can't remember what it's called. You put the bottle flat and spin it. Whoever it points to has to do a dare. Have you heard of it?'

'Of course,' he said, still frowning. 'But what if it doesn't land on either of us?'

'We cut down the middle. Whoever it's closest to.'

'Not what I meant.' Jonny shook his head and sat down beside the mirror. 'I suppose we're doing it here.'

'Might as well.'

'There're no parents around. Does that make dares harder or easier?'

'Depends,' I said.

'No neighbours. Nothing to Jenny.'

'Fine.'

'Because there was that time.'

I frowned.

'With the old table with the hole in the middle.'

Bursts of air hissed between the sides of my tongue and my teeth as I tried to suppress laughter.

'It was a dare,' I said.

'You put a ruff over the hole from the dressing up box, and told Jenny to sit on a stool underneath with her head through it!'

I stiffened at his accusatory tone.

'It was only a joke.'

'But it was funny!'

'No it wasn't.'

'You were laughing a moment ago.'

'Jenny just sat there. We forgot about her. Mum said two hours.'

Jonny rolled over backwards.

'You were worried about her a minute ago!' I said.

'It wasn't me who served her up on the dinner table!'

He saw me staring at the ground with my hands on my hips and the laughter passed from his face.

We were quiet for a while.

'It's going to rain soon,' I said.

'Stop making stuff up. It's sunny. Let's play this game.'

I placed the bottle in Jonny's outstretched hand. The wind pushed its way through the garden again, and I put my collar up, felt it fall flimsily down. I thought I might run for a jumper after all. The mirror on the ground showed the same sky as before: darkening blue with pink clouds.

Although I strained against it, I felt a muffled ache in my stomach. If Jonny felt it too, it did not show. This was the first time we had been left to look after ourselves. That was how Dad had put it to me, but I sensed he had said something else to Jonny. I thought of Jenny sliding out of sight in the window frame. A sliver of cloud moved far beneath my feet.

'I'm going to check on her.'

Jonny nodded solemnly.

I ran up to the house, through the kitchen door, pulled my favourite jumper from the back of a stool.

'Jen!'

Jenny was sitting in her bedroom reading. She stared at me

when the door slammed open.

'Knock,' she said.

'Excuse me.'

I curtsied. Jenny turned calmly back to her book.

'Do you want to play with us?'

'No thank you.'

'You don't want to?'

'No.'

'Will you be all right?'

'Yes.'

'How will we be able to tell if something's wrong?'

Jenny looked up and straight ahead.

'If you don't see me I'll be fine.'

'If you don't tell us you're not?'

Jenny nodded.

'Done,' I said.

Jenny's white dress had pooled around her as she sat. Strands of her blonde hair burned like filaments in the light of the window. She looked like Alice in Wonderland.

'Don't disappear down any rabbit holes!'

The corner of her pale mouth flickered.

I found Jonny tapping the bottle on the mirror's surface. It flashed green in a whirl of light and shadow.

'Let's play, let's go!' I shouted, clapping my hands.

Jonny rolled his eyes, caught the bottle at the neck. It seemed to be lit from inside.

'If we must.'

My thoughts thinned suddenly, became blade-like.

'Cheer up,' I said.

'Less talk, more action.'

Another phrase of our father's. The bottle was revolving again. It slowed to a standstill, poised equidistant between us.

'What are the chances,' said Jonny. He spun it again. It stopped, the neck pointing directly at him.

'Yes!' I cried.

'It's on you.'

'What?'

'We haven't decided which end is the main end.'

'It's the top, of course. So it's your dare.'

'No, we'll start again.'

He had already spun it a third time. It began to slow down.

'You – you – you!' I shouted.

Jonny shrugged.

'Whatever.'

'So.' I pressed on my lips with my forefinger. 'You have to run around the garden. Pretending.' I paused. 'To be a monster.'

'Trust a girl to come up with something like that.'

He stood up.

'Aren't you playing?' I narrowed one eye, carefully emptied the emotion from my face.

'This is a kid's game.'

'On TV they were much older than us.'

'Well, they were acting like kids.'

'They were grown-ups.'

'Well, they weren't playing the grown-up version!'

'What's that? We'll play that.'

'Oh, you wouldn't like that!'

'We'll play it. Sit down.'

Jonny stared at me, scowling again. He sat down.

'Well. Whoever loses,' he raised his eyebrows, 'has to kiss the other on the lips.'

'Yuck.'

'Told you.'

'I didn't say I wouldn't play.'

The bottle motored in the sunshine again. It landed on me. Jonny laughed maniacally.

'We can stop now if you like.'

I shifted the bottle round slowly with my finger.

'That's it. The bottle landed,' he said.

'I know. I'm just seeing.'

I looked at the ground floor window on the left.

'Jenny's there!' I said.

Jonny looked.

'She's just spying. We can stop if you like.'

I glanced quickly up at Jonny and back to the mirror. Then swung my foot out, pivoted forward, and kissed him.

Jenny banged on the window. She was crying.

'Jesus Christ,' said Jonny.

'Don't swear.'

My sister's loose hair swung from side to side. Then she dropped out of sight.

Jonny was lying on his back again. I remembered my jumper, slid it over my head, held the collar tight round my neck.

A sound from the street.

'The front door,' Jonny said.

'Jenny?'

He nodded.

'Gone to find Mum and Dad.'

A short time later, the door slammed again. I looked at Jonny.

'She's gone back in?'

'She probably just couldn't shut it properly the first time.'

I examined the back of the house, let my eyes rest on the window where Jenny had stood.

Inside the dim interior, it appeared as though a swarm of fireflies had become trapped, wheeling slowly through the shadows. I tilted my head. A far-flung galaxy.

'Jonny,' I said.

'What?'

'Look at that.'

I pointed.

Jonny sat up. He looked puzzled. The fireflies disappeared.

'Funny,' he said.

I was already on my feet. The ground floor window on the other side of the house was bright white. Nothing was now visible through two of the upper three.

'Jonny, the house is on fire.'

'No.'

Pause.

'Shit.'

'Don't swear. Jenny's okay?'

'She left.'

'What do we do?'

'Nothing. We don't go near it.'

'Really?'

'Really. Just sit back and watch.'

All the ground floor windows had blacked out now.

'It will take a few minutes to burn. We were playing. We didn't see it happen till too late,' said Jonny.

'The other houses.'

'We'll shout when the fire's obvious. We can watch in the mirror.'

I nodded. Without any sense of volition I turned and sat, stared into the mirror as Jonny pulled it up in front of us.

'Minding our own business,' he said.

In the mirror we saw our mother putting on her earrings. She sat at her dresser, gazed at something invisible in her fingertips, before her hands disappeared behind a sweep of dark hair. Her far ear flashed red and blue, sparked by a tiny diamond. Then she gazed at her fingertips again, which appeared to tremble slightly, a trick played by distance. She seemed to be finessing a magic thread. Then I stopped thinking.

We leapt up and shouted in unison, the garden turning around us, but although my throat was burning, no sound seemed to come from my mouth. The glass of the windows downstairs glittered as it gave out, flame churning in each casement, smoke found the sky and I ran until the heat seemed to hold up its hand to me. Dull white noise came from inside.

My mother's hair fell again to reveal one cheek effulgent in the lamplight, her long smooth nose, the slight softness around the deep lines in her face. Under kohl-black eyebrows, her hazel eyes moved up and to the left. She was listening. Put the earring down.

Sounds like an ocean moving in the distance. How funny! With Isabel flailing outside, opening and closing her mouth, as though she were drowning.

My mother had no way of escape and died in the fire.

For a while afterwards, I would picture the house cooling the following morning, misty still in the dank air and jagged like a razed forest. My mother would be lying in there somewhere, untouched by the flames.

She was asleep or I was asleep. Then one of us would wake.

I never saw the wreckage of the building. We left London the same night, heading for our uncle's house, from which we would move to a place on the edge of a village in Oxfordshire.

I remember the motorway at midnight, glowing orange. Jonny in the front, Dad driving. Jenny was beside me. Jonny guessed right: she had escaped.

My mother had left enough money for me to buy the small flat on the western edge of Chelsea that I moved into after university. I studied Art History at UCL. Both of my parents had read English at Oxford, and literature had always been my preferred subject at school, but the fact that my brain had always been awash with books, as well as my certainty that I could never better their achievements at Christ Church and Magdalen – Dad and Mum respectively – led to my spending three years studying paintings rather than words. The vitality of London drew me back there as well, I could see myself struggling in the rarefied air of an old university town.

Mum had been neither poor nor well-off, and when she married my Dad shortly after they graduated together they had lived in a basement flat in Hackney for a few years, piecing together the rent like a jigsaw. Dad had decided to become a literary critic. His family were rich, but believed he should find his own way, and I never heard him suggest that he had thought otherwise then, or did now. Their time in Hackney was a source of endless anecdotes, and the pressure of financial matters, weighted with a hard-to-imagine-future writing books, seemed to have created a perverse kind of peace within their poorly lit bunker, an audacious and rebellious calm. Anxiety was on all sides, but it wouldn't be allowed to wall them in. A corona of significance hovered over every idea and household object: short-term thinking was all they were capable of, but this increased the amount of hope they allowed themselves to focus on the present moment.

At least, this is how I imagined it.

Dad was writing a book of criticism – on what or whom, at this time, he won't tell – mocked by his tutor for stepping outside the safety zone of a PhD in order to do it. My mother was writing Naked Light. Dad worried about his stamina for the job. Mum told him early on that writer's block did not exist: there could only be a lack of patience on the writer's part. She said that if you don't have the patience to wait for ideas – if you expect them to arrive like clockwork every day – then there is a good chance that you should not be writing. Her ethos and stubbornness gave confidence to both of them. Their world was propped on her books like a table with a broken leg. At first, the faith they put in her artistry seemed justified. After Naked Light was published, the newspaper review pages became a tablature of their dreams, and they sailed west to the land of white stucco and wind-tossed trees.

'There's a chance that you should not be writing.'

Half of my life thus far I spent dodging bullets like this. Of course my mother never said such things to me directly – I was too young even for her prodigious literary admonitions when she was still alive – but through conversations with my father since I have learned both to respect and to despair at the force of the strictures that she brought to bear on him and on herself.

'Of course she would never have told anybody not to write,' he had said one day. 'Artists swing from competitive instincts, to a horror of extinguishing any measure of something so precious as a person's inspiration.'

'They take things to extremes,' I said.

'But they don't have a capacity to feel more intensely than the rest of us. They just choose to focus on their feelings, to draw them out to their most delicate lengths.'

'The rest of us? I've told you I'll write at some point.'

'Well then, I'll say to you what your mother said to me. She would advise a young writer not to make a go of things. That the rewards are not worth the trouble. And if they found then that they still wanted to, then that was probably a good sign.'

I am embarrassed to admit that I envied my mother the chance that having no money gave her to test herself. I've never had any intention of giving up my financial security, to take the same test myself. And so, a year after finishing at UCL, I had a head full of icons and canvases, the pale brickwork and glitter of the Fulham Road on my doorstep, and all the money I needed – money generated by my mother's creative success – to sit in the late autumn light each morning and wonder what I would do with the day.

I had a drawer full of half-finished articles on painters and photographers. I had thought that I might try to get some freelance work published in an art magazine that an old friend worked for, but each time I tried to write, I found that my energy would give out after a few paragraphs. Once I had introduced the key ideas, I did not have anything else to say. Then I would sit in a café nearby, go to the supermarket, empty on a weekday, read the paper, watch a film. Up until the end of university I felt that I had been moving towards a faint but definite point on the horizon. Now the horizon had disappeared altogether. I had always intended to do something brave, extraordinary. I had talked at UCL about writing a book on contemporary British art, and my tutors had encouraged me, but I knew I wasn't ready for such a task. And so I sat at home and waited, as my options began to narrow, and my life slowed to a standstill.

A strange fog had got into my head. I could no longer think clearly.

Newspapers stacked up, time seemed to flatten and shut me out: days do not drag on when you have nothing to do, nothing to think, nowhere to go. They flutter past you and discard themselves, until you begin to remember time being something cavernous you could lose yourself in. Avoiding eye contact with the cashier in cafés, standing outside the newsagent's while finishing a cigarette and turning away from the eyes of the passers-by, I felt as though, atom by atom, I was vanishing.

I tried not to panic. I believed that if I kept trying, with all my strength, to focus, sooner or later my vision would clear.

Halfway through November, my first visitor appeared.

I woke up late that morning, put on the clothes I had worn the day before. At my usual café, I sat by the glass front to watch the street, staring into the middle-distance when a black jacket blocked my view. Light brown hair, artfully tousled, fell across the girl's shoulders. She had her back to me, hands moving silently, working through her handbag, which I could see into from where I sat: a couple of books, a cleanser, hastily pushed aside. She straightened, reached around the back of her neck with her left arm, pulled her hair from the other side of her face. I caught a fraction of her profile, decided she was no older than twenty-eight. She thumbed the keys of a mobile with her free hand, ended the sequence on the red button. Looked from side to side, back at the phone. Pulled a cigarette from a snarled-up pack, then seemed to place it in her inside coat pocket, out of sight. She dialled again, lifted the phone to her ear.

The waitress put my coffee down.

'Your phone's ringing.'

I picked up. She introduced herself as Imogen Taylor. I watched her begin to gesticulate.

She spoke quickly, excitedly, said that she was studying my mother's work for her PhD at King's, that she needed to understand what my mother wanted to do with her writing, particularly in her later works, The Black Cloche and Midnightsong.

'I wasn't expecting you,' I said.

'It's funny you should phrase it that way! I was hoping I could drop by.'

'I'm afraid I live pretty far south-west.'

'Believe in coincidence? That's right where I am!'

I blanked, gave her my address, heard myself inviting her over. She disappeared. I left the café, hurried through the side-streets to my flat. The doorbell rang just after I got back.

'That was quick,' I said.

As she stepped in I caught a back-draught of perfume. She smiled, glanced at me and shrugged, walked through into the sitting room. Later, I decided that her eyes contained the blues you see in Titian's skies: azure and sapphire, peculiarly un-English, the colour of exaltation and vast distances. She did not look like an academic.

'What a beautiful apartment!'

I felt embarrassed. I began by explaining to her, from where I was standing in the hall, that her studies were doomed to fail. She had read nothing of Midnightsong, and it was likely to disappoint her. It was a smattering of scenes, barely connected.

She did not reply. I followed her into the front room, where she was sitting on my sofa.

'Let me begin at the beginning,' she said, smiling and looking at me sidelong, as if to say: I know what you're thinking, but it's a long story. I think this is as strange as you do, believe me.

I felt as though I was being enlisted. Designated co-conspirator. I shrugged.

'You're thinking,' she said, 'there's a stranger in my flat and she wants to write a book about my mother's books, and this evening was supposed to be a quiet one.'

Twenty-seven, twenty-eight.

'All I want is to talk to you about your mother. It might be fun. And who knows, you might decide to help me out after all.'

'I don't think so. This was a bad idea. I'm sorry.'

I walked out into the hall again, held my breath. And I would have asked her to leave then, had she not called out to me.

'Fifteen steps.'

'What?'

'Fifteen steps from the front door to the back door. Fifteen small leaps for you. And fifteen steps up the spiral staircase. The house in Belsize Park.'

I went back.

'How did you know that?'

'I suppose I won't take offense.'

'Did we know each other?'

'I used to look after you. When your parents were out. Babysitting.' She corrected herself. 'Childminding.' She shook her head. 'You really don't remember, do you?'

'No.'

'Jonny, Jenny and Isabel. The Sykes kids! We played rounders in the garden.'

We had played rounders in the garden. But I didn't remember her having been involved. We had a string of young babysitters. I couldn't remember all of their faces, so it was possible that I had known her. She was smiling on one side of her face.

'What else?' I said.

'You could hit the ball harder than Jonny. He didn't like that.'

True.

'You have a scar on your left knee. You fell over outside the house one afternoon. It was spring. You wouldn't let me pick you up. Afterwards, you said the light was like diamonds. How am I doing?'

I remembered, vaguely, falling over outside the house on the street one spring evening – but this could have happened hundreds of times. The dim face of an older girl, who was looking after me, peering overhead. It was my birthday. I was wearing a hated pink dress.

'What colour was my dress?'

'Your favourite colour was blue.'

32

True enough. I paused.

'So you knew my mum.'

'Hardly. I lived round the corner. I helped out a few times.'

'Which street?'

'Off Fawcett Road.'

'My way to school.'

'Exactly.'

'And you want to ask me some questions about her.'

'I thought we could help each other. I've always had the deepest sense of connection with her work. I mean, I think I understand it deeply.'

'There are lots of books about her.'

'Do you think there are any good ones?'

'No.'

'Exactly.'

'You don't look like a critic. I don't mean to be rude.'

'Like a babysitter?'

She laughed. She leaned over herself slightly, sitting forward on the sofa, straightening her back every now and then and holding the position before relaxing and leaning once more. She was beautiful. Her face had an unreal quality to it, a harmony of proportion that slowed the dexterity of my thoughts as I tried to make sense of her.

'How would I know?' I said.

Her clothes were immaculate. Skinny jeans, soft black leather boots and a pale green cashmere sweater showing under the black wool jacket. Her voice was melodious and well-pitched. She suited my shiny flat better than I did. When I needed new clothes I chose them carefully, but I had grown up terrified of girls like this. When she had looked after me, I must hardly have spoken, I thought.

And yet she had difficulty making eye-contact: her eyes would lock onto mine, then slide across to fix on a nearby object for a time, as if she were viewing me through a mirror.

She returned to the beginning of the conversation.

'Everybody knows that when your mother wrote Midnightsong, she became reclusive.'

'Everybody.' The hardness in my voice came automatically.

'Sorry, that sounds crass. I'm not forgetting that I'm talking to her daughter. What I mean is, I need to get a sense of how she was as a person then. To try to understand her need to seclude herself. What makes somebody lock themselves away like that?'

'She always isolated herself to write.'

'But to such an extreme degree.'

'I'm not interested in biography.'

'Neither am I.'

'Then what?'

'I need a sense of mood. Of atmosphere. To see if my instincts as regards the essence of the person are correct.'

'You want to capture her soul?'

She laughed again.

'No. It's like this. I knew her a fraction. But I need to feel as though I knew her personally. Not to suggest that there can be a through-line between her life and her work. But – it's like this.'

I waited.

'This will sound presumptuous. But I want to feel as though I have a right to write about her work. Not just for professional ends. I fell in love with your family during that spring and summer. And I've always felt that your mother and I were on a similar wavelength. She would talk to me in the kitchen when she got back late with your Dad, after he'd gone to bed. I would ask her questions about what it was like to be a writer. I had no idea that writing would be something that was possible for someone like me, of course. We had conversations that lit up my world, gave me a sense of the possibilities out there. "The shadows of the day, the fire of the night."'

An okay line from one of my mother's early short stories. Imogen Taylor was trying to show that she deserved to be here. To be asking this of me. What, exactly?

She was still talking.

'The idea began when I discovered this journal of mine among some old boxes at home. There were a couple of months back then when I followed your mother... she had told me that she was exploring the city a lot at the time, looking for inspiration. It was while she was writing Midnightsong. In my naive way, I wanted to know what looking for inspiration was like, so I followed her and kept a record of her movements.'

She looked at me directly as she said these last words. An apology and a refusal to apologise. She had expected that I would be offended by her admission, so I focused on my curiosity.

'And?' I said.

'I couldn't reread it all. Reading the first instalments, I was reminded of how unsettled I was when I wrote it. So I stopped.'

Her eyes fell on a book that was lying now in front of her on the table, bound in a black hardback cover.

'Can I have a look?' I asked.

'You could. If you wanted to. But I'd advise against it for now.'

Again, the direct eye-contact, quickly broken off. I had to laugh.

'What could it possibly say?'

'Reading it felt like sliding into something.' Her eyes found a candle on the table to look at. 'I've thought about this. It's like when you're walking along your own street at night. You've known the neighbourhood for years. But something in the air isn't right. Nobody is around. The cars are lined up as usual. The street lights are on. The leaves of the trees are like bits of gold leaf, they don't seem to be joined up. As though they all might flutter suddenly to the ground, along with everything else. Something like that.'

She frowned, as though trying to remember how she had started. When she began again, she spoke more quietly.

'Does this make sense? Something in your mother's actions evoked this kind of apprehension in me. So I stopped following her. I shut the book. Turned back.' She shrugged. 'It was as though it were me who was being followed.' She nodded for

a while, as though to herself. 'I want you to read the journal when we know each other better. When we can really discuss it.'
Eye-contact.
'Maybe you'll trust me enough by then to let me read Midnightsong'.

My first conversation with Imogen unnerved me. I had not asked her any of the questions one might normally feel compelled to ask a stranger who arrives at your flat and asks to be let into your past, to hear the stories that shaped you and that bind you to your mother.

Despite myself, once she had left, I realised I was eager to help her out. I wanted to learn more about her. She had left me feeling unsettled, but in the same way that a sun-flecked alley, branching from the route you follow every day, does: you wonder how you failed to see it before, and what might happen if you were to step off your usual path and follow where it led. Something like the buzz of playing truant. I became excited about seeing her again, happy to forget about the journal for now, if that was to be a rule of the game.

The next time Imogen came to the flat, she told me what she thought of Naked Light. The conversation, as before, felt awkward, and she expressed her thoughts on the book in a cursory way that suggested she understood it as well as she cared to, that it no longer presented much of a puzzle to her. Naked Light is the only book of my mother's that still receives universal acclaim, and no doubt that has much to do with the way that it welcomes the reader into its world, presenting the story to them in a clear way.

The geometric hedges and lawns of the great garden at

its heart shift in a heat-haze, as though underwater. The working title for the book was Neptune's Kingdom. By the time Celine Curtis has been discovered dead, drowned in the basin of a drinking fountain in the depths of her fiancé's family estate in France, we have seen her broken by disturbing whispers and rumours about her engagement, echoing through the château she has journeyed to. We have watched the lovers wander through endless networks of paths and colonnades, minded of small fish lost in expansive caverns, put up against a dark immensity. It was a beguiling murder-mystery.

'Your mother will often describe the backgrounds of scenes in extreme detail,' said Imogen. 'It's a key part of Thunder, Lightning. But it begins in Naked Light.'

My mother had once set me a challenge when I was younger: to look for clues to the meanings of paintings by studying their backgrounds. She had cut out perfectly formed black shapes which obscured the main objects of the pictures reproduced in books. I distinctly remember the game, not only because I continue to be amazed by the intricacy of the black paper shapes when I call them to mind, but because I was unable to come to the most distant understanding of what my mother wanted me to seize upon.

I have since asked my father about it.

'I once found your mother staring at the bottom of a painting by Titian during a visit we paid to the National Gallery in Edinburgh,' he said. 'Diana and Acteon. Below the commotion caused as Acteon crashes into the midst of the company of nymphs, who rush to surround Diana and protect her modesty, the waters of the river are sifting the sunlight of the forest clearing. It was in this movement that the world within the frame came alive for Marianne. These were the waters, she said afterwards, that would pool to show Narcissus his face. That had engendered the nymphs that crowded the picture. The depths suggested there added a new dimension to the work and ensured that we saw a whole world, not just a scene from it.'

'I think I understand. You might find more stories if you followed that river.'

'Exactly. You might find the rest of the universe, the cosmos. So she told me. On a trip to Florence, at the Uffizi, I found her gazing at the flowers at the feet of the women dancing in Botticelli's La Primavera. Strangely flat, upright. They look as though they might be made of paper. I would never approach her while she was concentrating, but afterwards I asked her, "What about those flowers?" "The way they were patterned," she said. I have looked at reproductions since, but can't claim to understand exactly what she meant that time. But I think she saw a kind of logic there that perplexed her. Can't do better than that.'

I told all of this, in turn, to Imogen. She made notes as I spoke. Eventually she looked up.

'So when your mum played games with you, they weren't the usual thing. That makes sense.'

'Well, it wasn't even normal for us to play games together. That seemed to be Dad's job. Mum was a writer, he said. She's working even when she's not at her desk. It was Dad's job to explain things as well, I guess. Although I was still very young when he said this. Sometimes his explanations didn't help.'

'He was trying, though.'

'Yes. Dad wrote about writers. The gift of creativity was as sacred to him as it was to Mum. He protected her from the world, and tried to protect her talent from it as well. She became very introverted. They had arguments. Eventually he became a target.'

'He became intimidated.'

'Sometimes I would think of the last time they were happy in each other's company. In my head I'd tie a golden thread from one moment of happiness to the next. Thinking something terrible might happen if I didn't. I'd imagine them dying in a car crash before they could make up again.'

'Most kids that age have no awareness of how their parents' relationship functions.'

'The basics. Arguing. Not arguing.'

'Have you asked your Dad if they considered – ' She paused. 'Spending time apart?'

I cringed at the euphemism.

'I doubt they did.'

She paused again.

'Sorry Isabel. I missed that a moment ago. Your worst nightmare came true. Something terrible did happen.'

'Not the worst-case scenario. They were blissfully happy all that week. And only one of them died. And...'

'And?'

'Nothing.'

'And it wasn't a car crash.'

She caught my eye and I laughed pretty hard.

Later, as the early evening outside the window turned the clouds lilac-grey and threw Brompton Cemetery into shadow, I set a cafetière down on the coffee table and we both lit cigarettes. I had agreed to tell Imogen the earliest significant memory I had of my mother.

The Playroom

Jenny turned to face me as I walked into the playroom.

'Why are you holding your nose?' she said.

'So the ghosts don't see me.'

She stared for a moment then turned away. She was shaking a doll upside-down. I began to circle her.

'That red dress is a bad sign,' I said.

She ignored me.

'How do I know you're not one of them?'

She stopped moving.

'I said, how do I know you're not a ghost?'

Jenny looked at me again.

'You might be one,' she said.

'Let's see. You're holding a doll, which means you can touch things. But the doll might be imaginary.'

'No it's not,' said Jenny, continuing to shake the doll.

'Of course it is. You're pretending to be a child.'

I heard Jonny's voice behind me.

'Don't cause trouble.'

'Sorry Dad.'

'I can tell Dad if you like.'

I pretended to ignore him, but I felt his eyes fixing on my back as I drew to a halt just behind my sister.

'Vanish! Be gone!'

Jenny put her doll down on the floor. As she stooped, her hair, seen from above, was like a pale blonde whirlpool, falling sheer to her shoulders. Darker regions dovetailed from the centre.

'Is that your real hair colour?'

I spun on the ball of my foot to face the inevitable reprimand head-on, but Jonny had gone. I weighed the situation in a moment: Dad would come up. Jenny was not crying. The situation was rescuable.

'It's a nice doll really.'

No answer.

'Why were you shaking it?'

Jenny stood and turned around to glare at me. A fragment of her hair was reflected in the cheval mirror behind her, along with a streak of red. Slowly, she withdrew an Alice band from her pocket. Pushed it back through her hair and stared.

'Because I wanted to.'

'But don't you want to imagine she's real?'

'No.'

I needed a smile. I danced across the room, past Jenny, to the mirror, ducked behind it. I extended an arm on one side of the glass and waved, before reaching around the front with a grasping motion.

'Pleased to meet you,' I said.

Jenny saw a disjointed arm shaking hands with itself and giggled.

'Pleased to meet you!' I said, peering from behind the mirror so that half of my face was visible, at an angle. Jenny saw a triangular head floating in space and laughed louder.

I stopped, detecting a change of atmosphere in the room. The tone and volume of Jenny's laughter altered. Through the thick, warm air that normally smelled of shampoo came a new smell, perfume, like a pristine melody.

'You're laughing.'

Mum. I stayed still.

'I thought you were upset.'

She spoke softly, almost whispering.

'Isabel is behind the mirror!' said Jenny.

'No I'm not!'

Jenny laughed again.

'Oh,' said my mother.

I jumped out. Mum was stroking my sister's hair, smiling blankly.

'Ah-ha,' she said.

They stood together in the doorway. I felt embarrassed, began to smooth my skirt. It was printed with small daisies. I decided that I did not like it very much.

'Look at me, Isabel,' said Mum.

I looked up.

'Do you still like that dress?'

'Yes.'

'You look lovely in it.'

I looked down again.

'You haven't been crying at all, have you Jenny,' she said. 'You look fine. Jonny said – '

'He's a liar!' I cried.

She frowned.

'What's that on your sleeve, Jenny?'

'Chocolate.'

'Maybe you should change?'

Jenny vanished. I had not taken my eyes off the pattern of daisies.

'You look lovely in it.'

I looked up at my mother warily. She wore a baggy shirt rolled up at the sleeves, the slenderness of her forearms exaggerated, hands motionless at her sides, pale, long-fingered against the darkness of the landing. I noticed her hair was ruffled on one side.

'Mum, your hair's funny,' I said shyly.

'Really?' She looked into the mirror across the room. One hand working slowly at her hair, she squinted, but did not move. She looked as though she had just woken up.

'Have you been swimming, Mummy?'

'Oh, no,' she said faintly, her eyes half-shut.

'I meant have you been dreaming.'

She did not respond.

'Tell me, Isabel,' she said distantly, as though addressing the mirror she was staring at. 'Are you kind to your sister?'

My palms burned. The playroom had become close, inhospitable. A heaviness settled in my throat.

'Usually, Mummy.'

My mother's hand closed on my right shoulder, her free hand grasping her own, her elbow resting on her chest.

'Good. That's what I wanted to hear. I'll be in my study if you need me.'

As she turned to go, I rushed to hug her.

When I opened my eyes, my arms were around her waist. She crouched to my level. I looked directly into her eyes. The pupils were finding their focus, tightening black circles that, for a moment, I could not make sense of.

'Isabel, I'm here.'

'I had a nightmare last night,' I said. I felt the need to make something up.

'Tell me about it.'

The dream was real, but had taken place weeks ago. I only remembered a small part of it.

'I was in the doll's house. The doll's house was in a dark room. And the stairs were broken.'

I felt my face flush and my mother frowned again.

'That sounds terrible.'

'Yes.'

'What did you do?'

'I woke up.'

'Well done. That's the best thing for it.'

'Yes.'

'Did you put the light on?'

I nodded.

'And read for a while,' I said.

'Everyone gets nightmares now and then.'

'You as well?'

I had asked my mother many times.

'Now and then.'

She stood up.

'Will you write about my dream?'

'We'll see.'

She smiled, hugged me, and stood up to leave.

'Mum?'

'Yes darling?'

'I'm not sure that I do like this dress anymore. I'm sorry.'

I wanted to keep her there.

'Don't worry about that,' she said, turning to go.

I looked at the floor.

The house was silent when I left the playroom and walked as quietly as I could across the landing, to the foot of the stairs that led to the door to my mother's study. I pulled my knees up under my chin, clasped my fingers around my shins and gazed at the thin bar of gold suspended in the darkness.

At first Imogen had sat awkwardly in my flat, but after we had spent many hours immersed in a haze of smoke and stories, she began to relax, become a part of the insular world that I inhabited. No longer leaning forward on the sofa, she would dim the lights, position herself wherever she felt like, sometimes sitting on the floor beneath the windowsill, wearing a halo of cigarette smoke, sometimes lying on her back across the sofa, legs flung over the arm. She would invent games, ever more eccentric ways by which we might reveal ourselves to each other, and usually she had her own way.

'When did you realise – '

'What were you thinking when – '

Insistently, she pushed me towards the most significant memories I felt I possessed.

'As you speak them,' she grinned, 'astonish yourself by thinking how different your answer will be, when I ask you the same question, months from now, when you've forgotten all of this, and I remind you what once seemed to matter more.'

I can picture her clearly one night having turned up in a pink jumper with two bottles of red wine, sitting back against the wall, locked in the light of a floor lamp as the cigarette smoke unwound around her body. Like her frantic conversation, it climbed into the darkness, conducted by her flicking, turning hands, encircling the room, re-emerged at the borders of the lamplight.

The stories that I told of my past catalysed our endless talks, stories that had begun to appear with breathtaking felicity, as though my command over the unseen parts of my brain was strengthening. A curious feeling of liberation took hold then, unsettling since I thought I had already mapped out the journey

I had taken through my life, but when it came to the events that felt like landmarks and milestones, Imogen encouraged me to find new through-routes.

'It's quantum physics,' she said. 'The same particle of matter can exist in many different places at the same time. It's only when we observe it that it seems to 'choose' one way to appear. Giving us a world that looks set in stone. But it isn't. And the past isn't many times over.'

As usual, she was several steps ahead.

'You're a Vishnu,' she laughed, 'skipping across the boundaries between the living and the dead.'

After every hour or so, I would go to the kitchen to fetch another bottle of wine and return to the half-lit sitting room, meet with an intense smell of smoke and bright perfume combined, which caused me to think that she must have been refreshing her scent when my back was turned – I sometimes thought I saw a hint of disgust when she paused before opening a cigarette pack – or that she was flushed with excitement perhaps, her rising skin temperature deepening its smell. Once we flicked on the main light and caught the jagged smoke hanging flat in weightless, timeless strata and she likened it to white noise, switched the light off.

'Steppes in darkness,' she said, settling back down beneath the lamp, face sfumato.

'Could you move across? I can't see you properly,' I said.

These evenings had traditions which needed to be respected, so that every moment would have the potential to be exquisite. How I saw her. What we drank and smoked. The rules of the conversation, of a friendship forming. The centre point of the evening, as in the Arabian Nights, was a request for knowledge. Once made, I would answer with a story, focus on her face, try to charm it. If she shut her eyes, I would be encouraged.

I told my memories of my mother as long, concentrated recollections. Sometimes I feared that secretly Imogen found my willingness to speak so openly about my life to be vulgar.

Then I would push for evidence of the same willingness on her part. When it suited her, she skipped across the surface of her own memory. Imogen coloured in her past for me whimsically, firing off anecdotes that dazzled, scattershot. I built up a fragmented picture of a life that was imposing in its limitless variety.

She would always return to her travels abroad. She would describe the view from a tower on the southern shore of Sardinia, the tower of a villa she had often stayed at with her family. She still did.

'The sea was like diamonds laid out on blue velvet.'

She would climb the twisting steps to the height of the tower most mornings, she said, before the others were up, with a shot of black coffee, look down over the barely stirring world. A white dressing gown protected her from the breeze which passed over the balustrade. I imagined the cotton flapping gently, the morning sky emerging from the sea. She would go there to be quiet.

Then came the sound of traffic. Paris fell from the sky. An open window framing the white and crimson awnings of the Quartier Latin, a grand salon in taupe and cream, the smell of myrtle confiture sweetening –

' – getting into the grit and fumes that my aunt let blast through the window. That particular aunt of mine, Susan, was born, she believed, with a French soul, but her enthusiasm for Paris was English. She'd marvel at the gravel at the Place des Vosges. She was massive, completely alive, in her own way. I remember a car journey with her, once, that began outside the house, that seemed to last only a couple of hours. Eventually the Brandenburg Gate rose up, history was happening, she said, and we were going to take a peek. The Berlin Wall was coming down. Could the Brandenburg Gate have flashed up? Could we have driven past it that day?'

'The day the wall fell?'

'No, it must have been just before. Anyhow, Dad had been

angry on the end of the phone. I remember seeing the guy hammering the wall on TV. I guess we stayed away from the crowds. In the end, I remember apple strudels. Unter den Linden. Chaos in the air, maybe smoke at one point. Paris is glamorous to a degree, but this was cake and revolution! Aunt Susan was in big trouble. Still, she had a cousin on the East side, and she could hardly leave me in France. Dad took me back to Berlin, eventually. Soon after Susan died. The wall was just a stripe on the floor then. We walked the length of it. After, I asked if he had found what he was looking for, and he laughed for a long time.'

She described a small café in Berlin where she and Susan had had fish for breakfast and to which she had returned with her father. I did not feel comfortable asking about this cousin, or her father's reasons for walking the length of the wall. No pause was provided to invite me to probe further. She joined separate points of light into constellations, too vast for me to discern.

I began to be curious about what sustained her soaring lifestyle: to put it bluntly, what did her parents do, how much money did they have, and how had her extended family managed to disperse themselves across the continent, the continents even, making the world an adventure playground for Imogen. Aunts, uncles and friends of friends seemed to await her arrival from New York to Mumbai. I felt that my interest in such practicalities did not compare well to the passion she felt for the emotional depths of my past. I kept my curiosity to myself.

'At the place in Sardinia, there's a garden with a fountain. I remember parking my tricycle next to it one evening. This was when I was really small. I got up when it was still dark, I couldn't bear not to be on it. But a snail had left its trail over the seat, all silvery, and I couldn't bear to get back on. Mum tried to clean it, I think. But I wasn't convinced. I think I had a thing about dirt. I used to be a nightmare when we went skiing. As you can imagine.'

She told me about her family's annual ski trips. She told me how the wind envelopes you when you ski, how you fear that your legs will wobble on your first steep slope, how you learn to relax so your legs firm up. I had never skied before.

'You seem to have spent your life on holiday,' I said.

She shook her head.

Once I managed to get her talking about her school. I had always watched the girls from South Hampstead on the streets around Belsize Park, in their yellow and black uniforms, talking quietly, seeming to float past just out of reach. Imogen made clear to me how boring she found the place, when the subject came up, how little interest she had in the people there, even though I gathered she was popular, hung around with the right crowd, as she put it, rolling her eyes. I asked about her parents – who I discovered she was living with, between flats – but she showed little interest, left them to busy themselves in the background, in a house with a grand name, twenty minutes' walk from the street I had grown up on, forever cooking fantastic meals, booking flights, opening doors.

'Why me?' I said one day. 'Or why my mother? I'm still puzzled.'

'Your mother was a genius,' she shot back. 'And I like you.'

One night, she told me about a bike ride she had taken with friends from school through fields of corn or something like it. They pedalled 'like crazy', careering from the paths, falling off, unable to push through the dense crops, scrambling back up. It was a hot day: the sun seemed ever-present in Imogen's memory. Finally, they came to a reservoir, 'or a lake, or a quarry,' changed into their swimming things.

Imogen's lips tightened.

'We messed around for a while. Then someone realised that one of us was missing.' She fell silent. 'I think I was stung by a bee.' She shrugged. 'I don't want to talk about it.'

'Is everything okay? You can talk to me.'

'I'm fine.'

I told her the story of the house fire. Once again, I saw the house burst softly into flames in the evening light.

'It's crazy to think of that house,' said Imogen, 'blackened and caved in. Like a rotten skull.'

'I suppose you must have seen it.'

'Sure.' She nodded. 'I saw.'

She was sitting beneath the window, one leg pulled up on which she rested her elbow, her hand holding the weight of her head.

'It's funny.' She lifted her face up. 'When I think of your house, looking at it before then. I always used to feel a kind of awe.'

'Come on.'

'Seriously! Things were happening inside that were extraordinary. Your mother was a great novelist, the mysteries behind her making those books, a book maybe being written right then – it was tantalising to me.'

'In what way?'

'It reminded me of a place in Sardinia – '

I had lost her again. She had made much of the wonder she felt towards my mother before, but here I had my first real sense of hitting something off-limits. However, I was soon surprised once more.

'I remember lying in bed the night before my first trip over to babysit. And thinking of your house. I already knew it. I spotted you all, one day, coming out for the school run. I remember trying to name the trees at the front, and getting nowhere. Apart from the cherry blossom. It faced the sun in the morning, didn't it?'

'I can't remember.'

How strange, I thought, to picture this girl, the hero of adventures across the world, staring at my house, as though it were the glittering end of her journey.

'I hope we didn't disappoint,' I said.

'I can't remember if you did or you didn't.'

Her fingers ran the length of an unlit cigarette. She examined the embossed crest on the box.

'You fetishise those,' I said.

'Sleep knits up the ravelled sleeve of care.'

'What?' I laughed.

'Thanks,' said Imogen. She smiled and snapped her lighter.

Imogen decided to stay over that night.

It was three in the morning when, after a few minutes of silence, I realised she had fallen asleep with her head in her hand, elbow still propped on her knee. Some part of her brain must be wide awake, I thought, keeping balance, still whirring beneath the torpor of the alcohol and the nicotine, the tug of exhaustion. She stirred when I patted her back, nodded, 'I think I'll stay,' let me guide her to the sofa, which unfolded to form the guest bed. When she lay down she fell asleep fully and I covered her. I stood for a short time, looking at the way her hair swept across her ear and cheek, become weightless in sleep, before switching off the lights and shutting my bedroom door.

The smoke had crept into the room and the pale yellow of the street lamp outside passed through the string holes of the blinds, laid a string of jewels across the duvet. Tonight, I found I could barely move, and lay across the covers fully clothed. The occasional bus heaved along the periphery of my hearing. Although my body quickly became dense, too heavy to lift, I found my mind would not be calmed, was colour-ridden and alive, lurching at times in the direction of sleep, before jolting me back.

Through the confused signals, a picture began to amass. Thousands of small spots of white, drifting forwards like flecks of foam on a slow-moving river. But the spots seemed to fall away as well, as though sinking into the water. It was as though I hung by my feet, watching the delicate shapes drift away in front of my upside-down field of vision. I heard my mother calling, softly at first, and the white spots seemed to quiver in response. I heard a strain of panic in her voice as the volume rose and felt a pressure in my knees, a quick wind numbing one side of my face.

My adult body jerked and I breathed deeply. Gripped the window frame and leaned out further over the snowfall... Something was rushing up behind me and I was about to fall.

The second time my body jolted, I sat up straight. My hands were trembling, I drew them in, held them under my arms. I'd lost any sense of how long I had been lying down. The room was cold. I got up and turned on the thermostat. The flame came alive. I pushed my way back under the duvet. Silence returned to the room and I began to empty my mind of its contents. I tried to let the thoughts that passed through go without touching them, letting them leave undeveloped. Before long, I would think about being calm, peaceful – still thinking, but conducive to sleep.

Some time later, still lucid, I heard a faint cry come from the sitting room: wordless, but it changed the silence. The dumb exclamation of the mind and body lost in sleep, identifying themselves to the darkness from the top of a steep precipice. Imogen's okay, I thought. Just a bad dream. She would not thank me for waking her.

Shifting my weight on my shoulder, I wondered why the thought of waking her had ever occurred to me. Perhaps I was jealous she was out of it.

The door handle began to turn.

I shut my eyes. No sound followed the creaking of the door and the handle gently knocking the wall. Eventually I opened them a fraction. A silhouette stood in the doorway, paler than the murky hall beyond. Shut them again.

Was she awake? Thinking of waking me? If not, I knew it

might be dangerous to wake her. I decided to lift my head a little, to adjust my pillow, a signal to her that I was awake, if she was too; but the figure in the doorway did not react and I resolved to keep still again. I had no way of measuring how much time had passed when eventually the door clicked shut.

Dad called the next morning. We arranged to meet for lunch.

'Somewhere quiet where we can hear ourselves speak.'

Imogen had gone. The sofa was back in place, sheets and blankets folded in neat squares on one arm, the sitting room aired, the washing-up done. The ashtray shone by the sink. A note was positioned nearby, carefully aligned with the edge of the sideboard:

'Up early – restlessness in evidence – and away! Will call. Imogen.'

The past night unfolded in my mind, Imogen's bottom lip grazed with wine, the light falling in yellow pearls across my bed, Imogen at the door to my room. The sequence ended with a rush of embarrassment.

I reread the note. She had been asleep, I decided. Only the ghost of a motive had put her on her feet. I grabbed my keys, touched the ashtray on my way out. Still warm.

It was late Saturday morning, the Fulham Road a rush of English and French. The bright blue sky scoured my eyes. Dad was waiting in a café with slate floors and white furniture, his face flickering with amusement. Waitresses sailed between swing doors. One was tilting a board lined with rectangular cakes in his direction.

He gave me an apologetic look as I approached, stood up to give me a hug.

'Let's have coffee then get lost,' he said.

We sat down and he looked at the table.

'How's work?' I said.

'Today I feel the need to retain some level of intrigue on that front. It may help me to maintain my status.'

'Meaning?'

'I'm sure my children have surpassed me in most respects. Jenny is leading an active social life at Bristol, to put it mildly. And your brother's quit his job and jumped on a plane, an experience I never allowed myself. He's had the original thought of travelling in Morocco.'

'For how long?'

'Indefinitely.'

Jonny worked – or had worked – as a solicitor at Freshfields. I pictured their office building as a giant glass cube. I tried to imagine him at his desk, but the cube would not let me in.

'He's muddling himself. Not that you could tell him that.'

'What's he going to do there?'

'He'll have all kinds of adventures.'

'What do you want me to do?'

'You could do the unthinkable. Call him.'

I smiled and shook my head.

'If his mind's made up, who am I to argue?' I said.

Dad fingered the lapel of his jacket. His white shirt collar and the V-neck of his jumper came together with geometrical precision. He would shrug off any compliments about his clothes with graceful insouciance. He had worn the same cologne for years – the notes of cedar and lavender reached me through the saccharine smell of baking – but he claimed that he could never remember its name.

'How are you, Issy?'

'Still trying to decide what comes next.'

'Sounds sensible to me. Take your time. Get it right.'

'Doesn't sound much better than travelling though, does it?'

'Completely different, your brother's approach to things. One can think clearly when one's mind is empty, so to speak. You can wait for what's important to make itself clear. There's clarity and focus. Not trying to move in lots of directions at once.' He traced a crescent of spilt coffee with his thumb. 'You're right not to succumb to that traction which pulls people of your age forwards at a crazy pace. As soon as you start to succumb to that pressure, you've lost.'

'Lost what?'

'You've got to keep hold of the thread of your own story. See the big decisions coming clearly. I'm talking in clichés, aren't I?'

I laughed.

'I don't need convincing. I wish I knew what I should be doing,' I said.

'Well, quite. But you're in a privileged position.'

'No rent.'

'You can tick that off.'

'No job.'

'No reason to worry.'

My father meant what he said, but I felt a certain pressure being exerted nevertheless. I reminded myself that he had not enjoyed these privileges when he was my age.

'Maybe I'm wasting what I have. What Mum gave me.'

'Don't apologise for yourself, Isabel.'

He beckoned to the waitress.

'I suppose we had better have some of those cakes,' he said. 'Just to check they are as sickly and unhealthy as they look.'

'I've made a new friend,' I said. 'She's called Imogen. She's really into Mum's work.'

'What does she do?'

'She's studying for a PhD. About Mum.'

'She's a reader.' He paused. 'So you're getting out a bit.'

'Kind of. She comes over and we talk. I don't go out much.'

'I'll let you in on a secret. Neither do I.'

'You're a writer. You're not supposed to.'

'Nothing wrong with spending time by yourself, either way. Don't feel bad about that. Sometimes it's necessary. But you're keeping your friends in sight too.'

'Her life story is crazy. What I know of it. She seems to have done everything.'

'Super-inspired? Relentlessly driven?'

'Yes.'

'Well, be careful. Remember what I said.'

'I find her inspiring.'

'That's a good thing.'

'She seems very creative.'

'Then you'll have a lot to talk about.'

His fork was now poised over a shining block of opera cake.

'Just find your own rhythm, Isabel. And trust it.'

We ate in silence for a while.

'Is Jonny happy?' I asked.

'Does he want to be?'

He paid and we walked up to South Kensington, where we spent the afternoon in the V&A. Dad said goodbye outside, made me promise to call him.

As I walked home, I felt unsettled by our chat in the café. I had been reluctant to mention Imogen. Something about our friendship seemed hardly to make sense when I said her name, sitting across from my father. Or perhaps I was unsettled by the way that my mentioning my mother went almost unregistered by him. I reminded myself that he would only talk – quite freely – about her once he had framed the conversation himself. Perhaps I had made a mistake by introducing her as a topic alongside an unfamiliar name, and now he was forced to imagine me discussing the woman he loved with a stranger, the blurred recollections, the inevitable inaccuracies, the misunderstandings.

I wondered what had motivated Jonny to leave his job and set off for a foreign country. With him I had no intuitive sense of when I could call him, when he might not mind being disturbed. I had gone to a party at his flat a few months before and we chatted briefly, got on well. Then he was laughing constantly, almost unrecognisable, not the young man with the melancholy turn of mouth and the slow-burn temper I was used to seeing with the rest of the family. Then again, ever since he had been a boy, his humour had always sparked suddenly, collapsing your understanding of his mood.

I tried to place him in Morocco. Out on a high plateau, overhead stars, soft blue rimming the distance: I could just about do it.

I called Imogen as I walked and she picked up on the third ring. We chatted for a few minutes, she said she had to go. Was she coming over tonight, I asked. She said that she was busy, it would be difficult. The line cut mid-sentence. I tried calling back, heard the fuzzy quiet of a misconnection. I said hello a few times, gave up. It had sounded windy where she was, her voice restrained as though she was with someone. Her family were gathered in the kitchen perhaps, Imogen sitting amongst them in one of those large old mansion houses, with golden squares of window light. They were laughing at one of her most infamous exploits, unwilling to let her leave.

I arrived home, put the heating on, piled up the newspapers and opened the bills I had brought up with me, before I realised that I was straining to see and flicked the light switch. I saw myself standing in the window, as though out over the night. Let the blind down. My legs felt slow and heavy. I turned on the TV and stared at the screen. The sound was off – I often kept it on mute in the background – but I had sat down now and could not bring myself to look for the remote. A panning shot of a bright room, small and windowless, underground perhaps, covered in ripped out magazine pages, cut to a blonde woman crying, shown from the shoulders up, long strands of hair sticking to the outer corners of her eyes. Her lips moved in a flurry, before opening and closing slowly, another flurry. A school photo of a small boy, grinning widely, began to enlarge, before a red bicycle appeared against a black backdrop. I got up and turned the TV off.

A plane droned quietly in the night, the noise flattening, louder now, spilling into the quiet. I spent some time listening to my own breathing.

Somewhere out there, a small boy was trapped, alone. Perhaps he was already dead. I was free to do as I pleased, but I was too afraid to move.

Afraid of what exactly?

My phone gave a message alert. It was Imogen: 'Tomorrow!'

'I went to see a few friends.'

She was looking down at the street. I tried to gauge her mood, to guess what she might be thinking. I pictured her up in her tower in the villa in Sardinia, staring out to sea.

What was she like with these other people?

I sat on the sofa and waited. After a couple of minutes she turned round.

'Let's have a drink.'

She sat across the coffee table, opposite me. I poured the wine. She peeled the thin strip of polythene from a new pack of cigarettes.

'I cleaned up,' she said.

'I didn't know what to do with myself.'

'You're lucky. Living on your own.'

I wanted to ask her about what had happened in the early hours of the morning, but my curiosity seemed inappropriate now. There was a quietness to Imogen, a sense of distance between us. After a short while, our conversation petered out.

She lifted her head and smiled, as though recognising me slowly.

'I'm tired,' she said.

'I can tell.'

'Please don't think me rude tonight.'

'I don't.'

'You're someone who is comfortable being quiet.'

'Sure.'

I was disappointed, but I knew what was coming.

'Tell me a story.'

She lay back in the chair, shut her eyes. For a moment it seemed to me that I was the visitor, and the flat was hers.

I already knew where I would begin.

The Study

Jonny turned his back to Jenny.

'Ready? Go!'

She took off, her lemon yellow dress flapping over the backs of her legs, up the narrow lawn towards the house. I could see the niche in her right shoe heel where a small golden key was concealed in transparent plastic. Blue above, green below: the stroke of yellow between gave me an incomprehensible feeling of happiness.

From where we stood at the end of the garden I could see my father on the terrace, bending over a camera on a tripod. A cloud's shadow fell over him, he seemed to drift further away. The curtains at the edge of the window over his shoulder began to move together slowly. Jonny looked at me and grinned. He waited until they were pulled tight then shouted:

'Coming! Ready or not!'

'The hall window,' I said.

'I know,' said Jonny. He ran towards the house.

I saw Jenny clambering onto the window sill, slipping behind the edge of the curtain, arms by her sides. She froze there, facing out into the garden. I began to walk towards the house.

'Issy!'

Dad was calling, waving an arm above his head. Quickening my pace, I arrived as the terrace emerged into sunshine like a ship's deck sliding over water.

'Will you stand there?' he said. 'I need to test the camera.'

'Why?'

'We're going to make a photo of all of us,' he said.

I spotted a cluster of crosses chalked on the paving stones, skipped over to the mark at the centre. Dad hunched over the camera again, fine-tuning the aperture and focal dials. Then he raised his head as muted shouting came from inside the house. Glanced at me.

'I'll go,' I said.

Dad began to raise his hand, but in a moment I was inside, heading for the stairs. As I reached the landing, my mother emerged from the bathroom holding Jonny's hand. He was shaking slightly, cheeks reddening. 'Calm down,' she said quietly. They passed me as though I were invisible, disappeared downstairs.

I stood still. The house was silent. Dust motes revealed themselves in the shadows. The same sense of peace that had permeated my body outside returned to me now. I thought of Jonny's damp face and felt myself drawing on secret reserves of calm. A mystery, then. On other days the sight of my brother upset would fill me with dread, and I would run to him.

The indistinct sounds of my family talking outside seemed to come from a different world, and I thought that I would try an experiment. I walked to the far wall of the landing, stood below the window that faced the road, and began to pace slowly – big steps – towards the window with the garden view. With each forward movement, I tried to detect a rise in the volume of the voices outside. However, since the person who was speaking kept changing, and the life in the voices grew and faded anyway, the experiment soon became nonsensical. I went into the room to my right – Jonny's bedroom – and pulled my head up over the sill before the open window. Here I could almost hear the others talking clearly. I climbed up into the casement.

'I'll go and get Jenny. She might fall.'

'She knows what she's doing. That's the work of an expert.'

'Still, Christopher.'

'Fine, I'll get her. What was the matter with him?'

'Oh, nothing. She wouldn't come down.'

'He's not like that very often.'

'Then it's like they forget to be upset.'

I could see the tops of my parents' heads. They looked like foreign creatures, far below.

I dropped to the floor, scanned my brother's room. The moment I realised that he would be angry if he caught me in here, another thought occurred to me. Pausing for a moment to check that I could still hear my mother's voice outside, I made my way back across the landing and crept up the second flight of stairs that led to her study. I was surprised to find the door ajar.

The room was bright and quiet. It occupied a small section of the top floor. One window overlooked the garden. From my vantage point, I saw only blue skies and white clouds.

I had sat at the foot of the stairs many times, listening for a ticking sound I could sometimes make out. I scanned the room, caught sight of an alarm clock on the window sill, the batteries standing alongside.

I took a step forward.

To my left was a chair with frayed upholstery, a pile of books at the centre of the seat. The desk, set against the far wall, was empty aside from a row of three silver pens and a shallow pile of paper, faintly ruled, the top sheet half-filled with tightly executed sentences. I peered over the pens, afraid to touch. They looked as though they were stuck to the tabletop. I strained my neck to smell the ink on the page, enjoying the rich chemical odour.

As I stood on tiptoe, I became aware of a hand holding something on the edge of my vision. Three large photographs, stuck side-by-side, had appeared over my mother's desk. The first was black-and-white, showed a hand reaching from the edge of the shot in the foreground, pale against a shadowed background, grasping the top of the back of a chair that was cropped just beneath. A small bright rectangle glinted to one side, apparently an open doorway in the recess of the room. I climbed onto the chair at the desk to get a closer look, taking care not to lean on my mother's work. I could discern half-hidden shapes in the dark around the door.

A woman's hand, I thought. The fingers, long and elegant,

curled gently around the wooden frame, applying just enough pressure to lift the chair, to pull it back, or to let go and leave it as it was.

'She's hiding,' I said out loud. Nervous to have spoken in the empty room, I challenged myself. 'Who's hiding?'

The next photograph, also in black-and-white, showed a woman whose face was partially hidden by the brim of a wide hat. Her dress came from many years ago, and her mouth, half-hidden, appeared to be smiling. She was sliding down a balustrade that sloped alongside a flight of steps in a garden, or at least pretending to. I noticed that, despite the fact that the bottom of her dress was swept up under her, she was crisply defined and her trailing leg was kicked up awkwardly. It appeared, then, that she was trying to present the illusion of motion, her fingertips pressed protectively to the edge of her hat. I looked closely at her hips, compared this point to the level at which the balustrade appeared from beneath her dress. She could not be sitting on the stone surface, let alone sliding. I looked again at her indistinct smile. She appeared to be levitating a little way above the world.

I turned to the final photograph.

Here was a brilliant, full colour picture of the earth seen from space. A special kind of photo, brighter than usual. I thought that the stars that clouded the edges looked like spilt flour, or a flurry of snow. Vague and distant when considered together, each by itself held a needle-sharp inner light, rendered with digital precision.

I was transfixed. I tried to imagine the distances that stretched between these points of light, that now seemed almost to touch. The sunlight dipped in the room again. The white clouds were swirling across the earth's surface, casting sudden shadows over my house somewhere below. The woman with the great hat was in her garden, leaning into space over the balustrade. And somebody was downstairs, the curtains drawn, about to pull a chair out to sit on.

My skin tingled under my hair. I wanted to grab one of the pens to write this down. But everything in the room was untouchable.

I felt a sudden lurch of panic, realised that I was still wearing shoes, jumped down from the chair, inspected the blue cushioning of the seat. No trace. I glanced back at the photographs, ran to the door.

In a few moments I was outside.

As I finished, I realised that Imogen was looking at me strangely.

'What about the ending?' she said.

'I don't follow.'

'Let me give you a clue. Your dad didn't take the photo.'

I stared at her.

'I would have thought I'd remember,' I said.

'I remember arriving that day and you were nowhere to be seen. I came to pick up a cheque. Marianne said your brother and sister had been playing a game. Jenny was dashing round the garden and Jonny was sitting on a chair on the terrace with a face like thunder. Your mum grinned. Don't mind him. She led me into the kitchen. I thought she was trying to remember where she had left her cheque book. She went upstairs. I looked at a picture that was up on the fridge. The Sykes family, painted in red, under a strip of blue at the top of the sheet, signed by Jenny. Why do children always have the blue so high up, and leave the white underneath?'

'Go on.'

'I paced the length of the hall and back. Counting the fifteen steps. Usually we did this together. Then I heard you screaming upstairs. Marianne told me she caught you in her study, reading a manuscript she was working on. She exploded. You bolted past me. I remember her thrusting the cheque towards me. Then Jenny ran in, told me I had to go out to take a photo. So I lined you all up. Jonny still looked cross. Your face was blank, like you were deep in concentration. And I thought I would've liked to be in that shot, standing between you and Jonny. There was something about these family rows that I think I found strangely comforting. I ended up staying until late evening, sitting on the terrace with your folks. Watching the three of you act out inscrutable dramas at the end of the garden.'

I saw it now. When Mum had shouted at me, I crept halfway downstairs, sat out of sight of the hallway. I did not want my brother and sister to see me crying. But I couldn't go back, out of fear of the woman who would come down those stairs eventually.

'You've got mixed up circuitry,' said Imogen. 'It's why you and I get on so well.'

'I don't follow.'

'I came to see you to find out about your mother. But you tell stories about yourself. And I hear about a little girl who's lost. Or looking for something.'

She looked down at the backs of her hands.

'Not the little girl I remember.'

I had always been honest when I talked to her. A sense of shame shifted in my stomach.

'I'm worried about you,' she said. 'You're always in when I call.'

The TV was spinning silent images. I wanted her to go.

And then I remembered the sound of rhythmic steps and quiet counting. I was looking down into the hallway of my old home. A shaft of light fell through the window of the front door, formed a white square that lay at the foot of the stairs, before the grazed mirror cooled and gave in to show a familiar ear, a familiar fall of hair. On the count of three, Imogen appeared, facing straight ahead. She continued to pace the hall, but I feared I'd been spotted. I wavered for an eternity, before running outside, one hand held over my eyes.

That night I could not sleep.

Sitting on the sofa, I felt nauseating contractions in my stomach. A pressure was building inside me, beginning here and gripping the back of my neck, speeding my thoughts up, giving them an unfamiliar momentum. I began to breathe deeply, pulling the air in, letting my lungs expand to full capacity. This eased the tension, stretching my diaphragm, but I soon gave up the hope that I would master the problem that night.

I turned the TV on again.

When I could not sleep, I would often watch the twenty-four hour news channels. One country's slow entropy, another terrorist atrocity and a child's disappearance. Everything whirling alongside everything else. It all seemed part of the same drama. When I was a child, at bedtime my mother or father would leave a small night-light on in the corner of the room. A sense of calm seemed to radiate from it. The pictures of bombed out cars and sobbing parents appalled me and moved me, it was not that I did not care. But, when I could not relax and the morning was a long way off, the bright pixels softened the night, the voices of reporters guarding against the silence.

When it began to get light, I boiled some water to make peppermint tea. I switched off the TV, soothed now by a placid blue that suffused the room. I remembered reading somewhere that electric light does not contain enough blue. It leaves something unquenched in the eyes of those who are keen on looking. Now my flat had acquired the fragile calm of a lake surface and, breathing the cool smell of mint, I found myself remembering the dumb sounds that Imogen had uttered the other night.

My phone flashed. So she had not slept either.

The text read: 'Sorry for what I said. I didn't mean to imply anything. Love, Imogen.'

I had already given words to what she had implied. Not her words to take back.

I was living my life alone.

The next night I wandered round the outskirts of sleep, into the kind of dream that troubles the half-waking. I saw rows of terraced houses outlined against a dusky sky, a pavement moving quickly, some white fabric, a handkerchief or a dress, passing across its surface. I stooped as I ran to pick it up, came to the shore of a lake, surrounded by rubble. Watched the fabric drift out over the water. The banks of the lake were strewn with abandoned factories. I walked towards the nearest. Steam began to issue quietly from monolithic mechanisms. The lake was gently shifting flakes of silver.

I walked into a forest and awoke.

The following days and nights telescoped into one another, barely brushed by sleep. I began to confuse the order in which I had carried out tasks, taken care of certain things, found it difficult to project more than one day ahead. My waking life was stealthily invaded by the uncertainties of night, passers-by rocked gently, rooms and streets began to blur a little.

Imogen did not get in touch.

I had picked up the phone repeatedly, made to tap her number and stopped, reasoning that she had caused some tension, last time she was here, that it was up to her to make contact. That she was probably thinking along these lines herself, but holding off for a while, adding a silent apology to her text message.

One morning I walked to the local café from where I had first seen her. I sat at my usual table by the window, ordered a double espresso and opened the paper. Exhaustion was exerting a pressure on the back of my eyes. I looked for a prominent object to focus on, to sharpen my vision, caught sight of Imogen's handbag at the end of the passage that led to the tables at the back. I decided I would catch her on her way out. After all, she might be with someone. The next time I looked up, the door was closing and a hint of red disappeared beyond the window's edge. The handbag was gone. I had been holding the paper up to my eyes, so she would not have seen me. Without pausing to think about what I was doing, I found myself counting to ten. Then I was out on the street, fixing on the red cardigan ahead, falling into step.

Imogen was walking quickly on the left-hand side of the Fulham Road, past the walls and the gates of private gardens. She passed the furniture shops and crossed the road at the traffic lights, turned down Old Church Street.

She stopped when her phone rang inside her bag. I stepped into a doorway. A boy on a push scooter skimmed up to me. I put a finger to my lips. He grinned and pushed on.

Soon Imogen was moving again, through a trellised archway, turning left along a narrow street under heavy branches. I kept a safe distance. As she took a right down an alley, I waited awhile, afraid she might have stalled round the corner. Then I crept forward, found it empty. After a couple of turns, it opened into a mews, crowded with low houses of various colours, stretching to a bend on the left, and a second archway fifty metres or so to the right. I looked at the houses, realising she might be inside one of them. Keeping my head down, I made for the archway, emerged onto a wider lane, lined with high walls and tall trees. The road was empty as far as it stretched in either direction, ending with a white wall at the near end, a glimmer of traffic at the other.

The tops of mansion houses were visible over the walls, chalk-white against the empty sky. I sat on a bench, and they vanished behind their defences.

What was I doing?

After a time, I felt a growing sense of anxiety. I didn't want to stand up again. Where would I go?

Imogen reappeared nearby. A boy and a girl followed her out of a black gate. They walked away from me, in the direction that seemed to lead to a dead end. Each child reached up, took one of her hands.

The boy was wearing a grey cardigan and scarf, socks pulled up to his knees. The girl was wearing a navy coat, twisting her long brown hair round her free hand. Imogen had changed her clothes: she wore a black skirt with tights and a jacket. She stooped slightly, they spoke quietly between crescendos of laughter, grew smaller and smaller as I watched. Laughter fading, they disappeared around a corner concealed at the end of the street.

I focused on the blank wall for some time after they had gone.

A few nights later, my phone rang at two in the morning. I was semi-conscious, half-dreaming again. It seemed as though my bed was in the middle of a corridor, and people I vaguely knew were passing by, peering over me, assembling and dispersing. I answered quickly, surprised by the volume of my own voice.

'Help me,' said Imogen.

The quality of the connection was poor again. It sounded like a powerful wind was picking up where she was, sucking the life out of her voice, a phone call from the edge of the world.

She did not say anything else. I cancelled the call, waited a moment, called back.

'Oh my God,' she gasped. Her voice was muffled.

'Imogen? Are you okay?'

'Isabel?'

'Yes.'

'I'm okay. I must have fallen asleep sitting up. How weird. Sorry.'

'Don't be sorry.'

'What time is it?'

'Don't worry about that. Just relax and go to sleep. Are you lying down?'

'Yes.'

'We'll have a chat tomorrow, okay?'

'The light's on.'

'Leave it in case you have a bad dream.'

'Bad dream.'

I hung up, pulled on my jeans and coat, left the flat, followed the Fulham Road back up to Old Church Street, turned right onto the side road. The trees here were studded with street lamps, branches breaking away into the black. I passed under the archway, through the unlit alley, along the mews, under the second arch and into the walled lane, stepped onto the bench, turned round. The buildings seemed to have been abandoned, apart from a room in the house next to the one in front of me. The curtains were drawn, but the window was lit.

Imogen was staying with friends, I told myself that night. Taking the kids out for the morning. Family, maybe. It was not a satisfactory explanation. Perhaps it was the way she was dressed, perhaps the way she bent down to talk to those children, laughing. I did not stop thinking about what I had seen until it was light, and a strange coincidence took place. A letter arrived, bearing a Moroccan stamp. As I came back into the flat, the phone rang. It was Jenny.

'Thought I'd get in touch,' she said.

'I haven't heard from you for ages.'

'Thought I might pay you a visit.'

I decided as we talked that I would sleep on the sofa, so I could access the kitchen and the TV at night.

'Next week?' I said.

'Sounds great.'

'Will it affect your studies?'

'I thought you might like to see me!'

She put the phone down. I stood with the receiver in my hand for a while.

Remembering the letter, I made a cup of tea, sat down at the table and began to read.

Dear Issy,

I hope all is well with you. I am currently in the town of Chefchaouen in the Rif Mountains. The weather is bright and chilly. I saw an eagle over the plains earlier. It was hanging in the air for hours. I felt as though it was a sign for something, but I would rather not know what.

There is an old man who lives in a house near where I am

staying who hangs brightly coloured fabrics out of his windows every morning. I cannot work out why. His son got into a fight yesterday with some young men, in broad daylight. It began with an altercation over money. The tallest of the group held out some notes and shouted at the man's son, who cuffed his hand, sending them fluttering down the sloping street. In an instant, they were all holding knives. An old woman passed between them, walking slowly. By the time she was gone, their blood must have stopped boiling, because they put their knives away. I had a horrible thought as I came away from the crowd: blood running all the way down the mountainside.

The old man was out the next morning, hanging his fabrics again. I think he must use his house as a shop. I will have a look inside soon.

I thought all of this might interest you. I thought someone should turn it into a story. If you did, I would love to read it.

The stars are like diamonds here. And it is freezing at night.

All the best,
Jonny

That night, I dreamt about fire.

Walking through the alleyways and streets around the Fulham Road at twilight, I was surprised to discover a small flame at the base of my thumb. I turned round and found my way to the house Imogen was staying in.

It was ablaze. I stood on the bench, strained to see whether she was still inside.

'I'm standing next to you on this bench,' said Imogen.

I turned to look at her. Her face flickered, eyes half shut. She held my hand.

'That's my bedroom,' she said, and yawned.

The Empty Pool

The flight passed in silence. Dad hired a car at the airport. It was a short drive around Florence to the hillside where our villa lay waiting. With each return over the years, it had taken on more magical properties.

'The castle in the sky!' I said, as the car slowed, the pale building appeared and the clouds seemed to turn towards us on the right. Further away, the rose garden flamed across a gentle slope.

'Mount Olympus!' said Jonny.

Jenny shot out the car, stood some way off beside the pool. 'It's empty!'

We gathered around the rectangular hole in the ground.

'It's deep,' said Jonny. The sun was decimating the weeds that had grown across the bottom.

'What shall we do?' I whispered.

'Let's have a think,' said Dad. 'We may have to call Dona.'

Dona was the ageing owner of the property who shuffled sideways like a crab.

'It looks like a lost cause,' said Mum.

'Let's have a think,' said Dad.

There was to be no swimming that holiday.

Jonny, Jenny and I played hide-and-seek in the garden, through the villa and as far down the drive as we dared, before Dona's house appeared around the edge of an orange tree, and we retreated.

A pipe had broken. The pool could not be filled.

On the third day we took the car into town. My mother mentioned the Uffizi.

'I want to catch the afternoon lull,' she said, and slipped away.

'What are we doing, Dad?' I said.

'We're going to have a wander.'

We walked between golden buildings, under a glass-blue sky. Jenny went to chase a pigeon in a square and we watched as a flock took off, swerved in the closed space. I pulled Dad over to a café, we sat and drank Cokes under umbrellas. The pigeons were harassing the passers-by.

'You disturbed the birds,' said Jonny.

My father was looking for the waiter.

Jonny leaned towards her and whispered.

'You're evil,' he said.

'Stop it!' I shouted.

My father's head snapped round. Jenny's face was crimson. She had spilt some of her Coke on her dress. When Dad looked at her she started to cry.

'What's happened?' he said.

None of us spoke.

Dad stood up and took Jenny by the hand. Jonny and I followed them across the square to a shop that sold hand-embroidered children's clothes.

'You two wait just outside.'

He disappeared with Jenny into a labyrinth of brightly coloured dresses hung on rails, and when they reappeared Jenny was smiling again. She was wearing a yellow dress patterned with poppies.

'Well? What do the two of you think?' said Christopher.

I could not decide whether I was being promised a dress in exchange for a confession, or whether this was supposed to be a punishment.

'Nice,' said Jonny.

'Do you have anything else to say?'

'I like the colours.'

I looked pleadingly at my brother. He shrugged and looked at the floor.

There was a storm outside that night. I lay on my bed, listening to the thunder. In between the blasts, I could hear my parents talking, softly but urgently, downstairs. I felt a sudden longing to be with Jonny and Jenny.

I slid down from the bed and went to the window, parted the blinds. A cloud lit up from the inside. It separated from its dark background for a moment before blinking out. Then the thunder arrived.

Even by lightning, the city could not be seen through the black and grey folds of the storm. As I strained my eyes, a troop of giants began to emerge from the deeps of the night, long silhouettes, clambering awkwardly towards the house. I watched them make ground before stepping back and closing the blinds, pressing my back to the sharp slats.

I shut my eyes and remembered a dream I had had a number of times now: I was stuck in my old doll's house, the stairs to the ground floor were broken. Frightening enough, though something much worse was about to take place. I always woke up just in time to save myself from whatever it was. Now that something seemed to flutter towards me. I shut my eyes, saw a switch on the wall in the doll's house. I pressed it. The darkness outside the windows vanished, I could see into the playroom, saw myself leaning in, one eye at the window.

'Stop it,' I said to myself.

'Isabel, are you okay?'

Dad was outside the door.

I kept quiet.

'I've brought you something.'

I ran to let him in.

He grinned, held up a blue dress covered in daisies.

'Thanks Dad!'

I hugged his leg.

'That's okay. I thought I would put it away for your birthday. But Jonny told me you didn't do anything wrong today. Then I thought maybe you'd prefer to have it now.'

I nodded vigorously. He sat down on the sofa.

'I'm sorry I was cross earlier.'

'I told him to stop it. At the table.'

'I know.' He paused.

'Did you keep my dress a secret to punish me?'

He began to fold his fingers together and straighten them. A butterfly appeared on his knee.

'Do you like it?' he said.

I realised my mother was standing at the door.

'Why is Isabel crying?' she said. She was looking at the arm of the sofa.

I saw that I was crying when she said so.

'I think it's because of the dress,' Dad said quietly.

She walked over to me and stooped to my eye-level.

'What is wrong with you?' she shouted.

'I don't know.'

She glanced at my father. He was watching me.

'What do you mean, you don't know?'

I shook my head.

I was sitting on the edge of a tall building, the slightest movement might see me fall. I pushed myself back into the corner of the sofa.

'Did you make your sister cry earlier?' said my mother.

I shook my head.

'Are you going to speak to me?' She paused. 'And what do you think of the dress your father and I bought for you, that cost a lot of money?'

I felt compelled to shake my head. Her voice rose again.

'Shall we put it in the dustbin?'

I kept still.

'Aren't you going to say anything?' she shouted at my father, trembling.

'Annie.'

The butterfly returned, opening and closing on his knee.

'I said,' she turned back to me, 'shall we put it in the dustbin?'

My mind was contracting, thoughts locking as they formed. I looked up at her quickly. She looked back from behind a pane of frosted glass.

'I don't know,' I said.

She snatched the dress and left the room.

I lay in bed. The lights outside my door had been switched off, my mother's shouts subsided. A new sound reached me: muffled sobbing. My mother or Jenny. At some point it dissolved into the clatter of the rain on the windows, quietening in turn until the house was silent.

I had decided to retrieve the dress.

Inside my holdall was a small silver torch. I took it out, flashed it around the room. Then I crept to the door, turned the handle slowly, stepped out onto the landing.

The torch light fell on a blue china vase that seemed about to tremble and break. Brightly coloured objects proliferated under the spotlight, as it wrapped around corners and alcoves. I felt sure that I had not seen many of them before, but now they seemed to jostle for my attention. I stopped at the end of the landing, shone the beam into a black bowl. Made, I thought, of the night outside the window. A running sheen swept around the depth of it as I moved my arm. Then, remembering why I was there, I turned the beam downstairs and lowered my feet to the base of each step.

I intended to search through the rubbish for the dress. Maybe my mother had pushed it as far down as she could, out of sight but not out of reach. I would find it. I pictured the mess, holding my breath, peeling plastic wrappers away from the fabric, bits of food. Then I planned to take the hand wash liquid from under the sink, that I had seen my mother use, climb on a chair and soak the dress till it was clean.

The torch light penetrated the hall and found the dustbin in the kitchen. I switched it off. The darkness protected me now. It contained some light that traced the kitchen doorway.

As I approached the dustbin, my mother spoke to me.

'Hello, Issy.'

I stopped moving. Her voice was soft and seemed to carry directly into my ear.

I turned round.

She was sitting in the corner, head and shoulders in shadow, legs folded in a wash of moonlight. Her raised foot was half-submerged in the dark, anklebone gleaming.

'Are you looking for your present?'

I nodded.

'Don't worry, it's not in the dustbin.'

I looked at the bin.

'I put it on the chair outside your room.'

'Oh,' I said.

'Isn't it nice down here in the moonlight?'

'Yes.'

I shifted my feet.

'Don't worry. This is the place where worries wash away.'

'What place?'

'It doesn't have a name yet. What should it be?'

'The kitchen.'

'You're smiling, aren't you? Let's call it the kitchen. Just for tonight, the whole world is the Kitchen. We could go out and take a look at it if you want. I see you've already got your shoes on.'

'I thought the bin might be outside.'

'Good thinking. I've got some candles.'

'What are they for?'

'Wait and see.'

My mother stood up slowly.

'Aren't you going to change?' I said.

'There's no need for that. It's even warmer out there.'

My mother picked up a box of candles from the kitchen table and opened the back door onto the garden, the scattered lights of the city's far edge, and a silent world of stars.

I imagined myself floating untethered from the hillside, the city gliding beneath my feet.

'Wait here,' said my mother.

I sat cross-legged and waited as she made her way into the gloom that blended with the night sky. Her figure broke up the lights on the horizon as she picked her way past objects invisible to me. She stopped. I heard a faint scratch, and a small flame listed upwards like a cinder on the breeze. My mother's ear appeared, hair turned blonde, the candle in her left hand lit.

I watched the flame sway, falling gently as she descended the slope. Immediately around her, a small shock of shadows splayed out like card shapes unfolding, the space between bushes incised by light, folding as she moved. The flame dropped suddenly and vanished.

I hummed to myself, looked up at the stars and thought about the constellations. They had always seemed like a trick to me, a cheap attempt to look for pictures that were not there. If anything goes, I would say to myself, I prefer to make up my own. I bent my neck, looking for the Milky Way. It unravelled like the train of a white wedding gown. A woman was running across the sky. She hid in the darkness.

When I looked down again, I saw a bright glow spread across the ground in the distance. I found my way through the garden, stopped a few metres from the edge of the pool.

'Can I look?'

'Ready.'

I inched forwards on hands and knees, looked in.

The bottom was lined with candles. My mother stood at the centre, hands on hips. She laughed.

'It's a camera lucida.'

'What's that?'

'It's a room filled with light.'

I darted over to the vertical ladder which ended halfway up the near wall. She lowered me down to the floor.

'What will we do in here?' I said.

'We'll sit in the middle and talk.'

We sat down.

'What shall we talk about?'

'Well, what are you thinking?'

'I'm thinking that I'm happy.'

'And what does that make you think of?'

I thought for a while.

'Of other things that will make me happy.'

'Things to come.'

I nodded.

'Of the future,' said my mother.

'The future.'

'What do you see yourself doing in the future?'

'Tomorrow?'

'And the day after that, and after that.'

My eyes widened. I tried to think.

'Lots of things! Playing. Laughing. Having fun.'

'And what about in the years to come? Can you see that far?'

'When I'm grown up?'

'Yes.'

'I don't know.'

'Too many things.'

'Yes.'

'Shall we list them?'

'I want to be in a circus. Dancing with horses. And music.'

'That's a good one.'

'Only I can't dance.'

'That's a shame! What else?'

'I'd like to be an actress. Then I could spend all day dressing up.'

'You could be a film star and travel through time.'

'Jonny says we'll all be able to do that soon.'

'Well, they think space and time are sort of the same thing, so if you can travel through space, maybe one day you'll be able to travel through time.'

'The same thing?'

'When we came here from the house, we moved forwards through space, and we moved forwards in time as well.'

'So time doesn't pass when you sit still?'

'Not when we sit in here, it doesn't.'

'Maybe I'll be a scientist! Then I can make a time machine. Why're you looking at me funny?'

'I like hearing you talk. Did you know that if you look along a street, you're looking backwards in time?'

I laughed.

'You're not!'

'Look up.'

We looked at the sky. The stars seemed brighter from deep in the ground.

'The light you can see, that comes from the stars, took seventy years to get here. Right now, you're looking back in time.'

'Is that true?'

'When you look along a street, you're really seeing what was there a moment ago.'

'Maybe I could be an astronomer. It sounds like being a time traveller.'

'A time watcher.'

'But not as fun as circus dancing.'

'With horses.'

'And music.'

'You never know.'

'You're looking at me funny again.'

'Don't be silly, Isabel.'

My mother leaned back on her hands, looked up at the sky once more.

'Thank you for bringing me here,' I said.
'No trouble at all.'

I sat up in bed, woke with my head tipped back as though surfacing from water. It was still night. My mother had led me to bed. The villa was quiet.

A soft groan came from outside.

'The giants,' I whispered.

I crept over to the blinds and opened them slightly. The moonlight insinuated its way into the room. The garden was a mass of black shapes, barely distinguishable.

There was a distant scratching sound.

I imagined a huge, sinewy leg stepping on to the grass. A hand sliding under the house.

It can't be giants, I said to myself, staring into the blackness forcefully. The fear receded a little.

The scratching again. I pulled my shoes on.

'Giants beware.'

The back door opened noiselessly. When the sound came again, I set off towards it, in the direction of the pool. The empty pool. No chance of any swimming this holiday. The pool that was usually so deep I could dive as much as I wanted, Dad said, that I would slide through the water and never touch the bottom.

The candles still burned, melted now to golden stubs. It took me a while to make out my mother, lying on her side below, arms wrenched out in front and behind as though signalling by semaphore, or, with bloody palms upturned, waiting to catch something that might fall from the sky.

I understood that she was hurt, in need of help. But, running back up to the house, I can only remember an alien sense of excitement, adrenaline shock. I woke my father. He moved with unreal calm and precision, lucid from the moment I woke him, asking questions, hitting the light, and I remember running from room to room, flicking the other lights on, as Dad spoke loudly in Italian on the phone, slammed the back door. I ended up in the small top floor bathroom, reaching for the light cord, sitting with my back against the bath.

Dona had insisted on taking my brother and sister and me in for the rest of the night. We sat in her sitting room watching TV, eating chocolate biscuits. Jonny waved her out of the way of the screen. My brother and sister thought Mum and Dad had gone to see the sun rise. Jenny giggled at Dona's chaotic lipstick.

In the morning, she bustled us into Mum's room at the Ospedale di Careggi, shut the door. I would not look at my mother at first. We could hear Dona's breath rasping in the corridor. Then the smell of cigarette smoke slipped into the room, followed by a reprimand shouted by a nurse.

Finally, Mum spoke.

'That pool was never as deep as your father said it was.'

Many critics claim to have found the beginnings of my mother's mental instability in her early work. Naked Light, of course, appears to contain a suicide. Celine Curtis is discovered dead, her body slumped over the basin of a large drinking fountain, face sunk in the water. Whether such an awkward form of suicide would be plausible is a moot point: unless she became unconscious as she leant over the water, we are forced to imagine her holding her face down in the font with horrifying willpower. The clipped trees that stand above her prone body seem to belong to a world in which such primal urges are obsolete.

Then there is the possibility of murder. Daniel, her fiancé, finds her at the fountain at the end of a shady walkway, says that her knees were bent too strangely, that she seemed to be about to leap upwards, was too artfully arranged, too carefully balanced for the theory of suicide to work. Killing herself that way would have taken staggering care and patience.

The heat has built to an unheard-of intensity over the course of the summer. Daniel's family are 'heliophiles': every party or gathering they host for the engaged couple seems to revolve around the sun.

Titi hauled his vast frame away from the crowded table – the rainbow–coloured cakes deliquescing in the heat – a Rorschach blot shifting into dog-shape, took a few steps, turned to shoot a bemused look back at the people laughing, sheltered by the great umbrella, caught Celine's eye instead. She jumped up, clattering a glass of iced tea, as Titi rolled on his weak paw and collapsed, struck out by the sun.

N.L.

Celine is a pale-skinned girl who has never left England before. Perhaps her lips did not reach the water in time, and like Titi, she felt the vicious effects of sunstroke. Or perhaps 'the sun sent her mad', as one of the visitors to the château decides. The rumours about problems with the engagement echo on, long after her death.

Those looking for the autobiographical angle in my mother's debut work, should bear in mind the fact that Naked Light was written many years before her more eccentric behaviour became pronounced, let alone her truly self-destructive episodes.

Thunder, Lightning comes a little later on the timeline.

A well-known essay, published a few years ago, focused on the possible links between the life of the protagonist of my mother's second book, Joseph Long, and her own. The argument centred on the scene in which Joseph is interviewed for a feature in the photography magazine, Wash. The conversation runs smoothly, until he is asked to discuss a small picture included in an exhibition of his in London, that seemed to have been passed over by most visitors, much to Joseph's dismay. He describes it as the key by which one might have unlocked the entire show. The interviewer presses, asking him to explain the importance of the shot, in detail. In accepting the challenge, Joseph breaks a cardinal rule which he has held himself to throughout his prodigious career.

It is a nocturnal photograph, in black and white. The composition will be familiar to readers of the novel: a black hillside cuts across the foreground, a second hill sweeps across the middle ground on the left-hand side, which the first hill overlaps. The second hill is turning spectral grey: a filament of lightning intersects the two.

He talks about the way in which the arrangement seems to expose the malleable nature of the world around us. At the right of the shot, the black hill merges with the night sky. The lightning comes from the dark to illuminate the earth, yet the earth contains the night as well. Everything is interweaving, like a scene from Genesis. The interviewer nods, scribbling notes as fast as she can write.

Since Joseph had always held the superstition that trying to articulate the mysteries of his art would weaken his grip on them, coupled with the fact that it's clear the finished article seeks to expose him as a fraud, it comes as no surprise that a period of self-questioning follows, before his self-confidence begins to deteriorate.

Frenzied self-examination leads him to withdraw from the world, and gradually Joseph becomes convinced he is losing his mind, or at least his talent.

Whatever animated me before, whatever force or patterning of mind it was that made me see the world differently, I have fallen away from it, divided against myself. Driving through towns and villages at night, I see other versions of myself, carrying a briefcase, sweeping a kerb, looting a cash register, each of these existences more real than my own, my solid life smashed into infinite possibility.

T.L.

Joseph refuses to take any more photographs. He and his wife are eventually unable to meet their mortgage repayments, his son becomes frightened of the glazed look in his eyes, and on the night that his wife resolves to leave him for an actuary, she discovers he has left her for Italy, where his extraordinary rejuvenation takes place.

The essayist who claimed to see my mother in the hero of the book failed to list the many differences between Joseph and his author. Focusing on his theory that my mother showed signs of psychological disorder at the same time she was creating Joseph, he overlooked the lucidity and self-assuredness my mother showed in interviews and in her professional life, when the public gaze fell on her after the novel's publication and its rapturous reception. Not to mention the fact that Joseph is analysed three times in the story, and each time given a clean bill of health.

The novel was released just before I was born.

After reading the essay on the subject, aged sixteen, I remember speaking to my father about it. He laughed off the ideas put forward, said the writer had missed a trick.

'In order to write effectively about a psychological state, you have to have risen to meet it, made yourself equal to it,' he said.

'So she did have the same problems as Joseph Long?'

'No. Your mother filtered her own experiences through her imagination, through her characters. Her novels were experience, changed.'

'But she may have been through something like what he did.'

'Well, we're all more alike than we think. And don't forget, Joseph Long wasn't mad.'

'He definitely wasn't? Did she tell you that?'

'Yes.'

It was something to hold on to.

Later that year, Dad took me with him to Gloucester Road to meet a biographer who was writing a book about my mother.

'Is it an official biography?' I asked.

He laughed.

Adam Sands – Dad explained that friends of his at Oxford, where Sands taught, had tipped him off – wanted to use the book to bring forward new evidence he claimed to have uncovered, regarding my mother's childhood, evidence, 'put bluntly, of abuse,' Dad said.

'What kind of abuse?'

'It's a surprise.'

'Is it true?'

'Not as far as I know.'

'How can we stop him?'

I thought I had come to see how a biographer worked, to get an insight into my mother's past.

'We'll stop him by letting him talk.'

'Maybe he'll say something interesting.'

'You can't write about the inner life of someone you never knew.'

I kept my eyes on the pavement.

Sands greeted us with a booming voice, grasped Dad's elbow as he shook his hand. Dad smiled back. Sands turned to me.

'Isabel,' he said, narrowing his eyes.

I held my hand out.

'Pleased to meet you.'

Sands questioned Dad eagerly about his lifelong love of Italy. Dad told him he was planning to hire an apartment in Rome to work in once his youngest daughter had been 'shipped off' to university.

Sands turned to me.

'I've got a sister,' I said. 'He's got a while to wait.'

Sands laughed.

'Jenny,' he said. 'Of course. Send her my regards.'

I can see now that my being there affected the entire course of the meeting. Maybe it was my father's way of telling Sands that the life of Marianne Sykes wasn't public property. When they began to talk about my mother's work, Sands started to bite his thumbnail.

'I was hoping to discuss The Black Cloche,' he said abruptly, 'in relation to some discoveries I've made about Marianne's past. There's no easy way to say this,' he said looking at me, 'but I have good reason to believe that the source of some of the material in the work may come from events predating your meeting, Chris. Evidence of family abuse. Frankly, I don't know whether this comes as a surprise or not.'

'It's not something she ever talked about,' said Dad.

'That makes life difficult, doesn't it?' Sands smiled. 'So I'll dive straight in. The physical and the psychological abuse in The Black Cloche.'

My mother's third novel was set in the twenties. Sarah Morgan, a young woman whose glamorous lifestyle ended with her husband's death and the birth of their physically handicapped daughter, finds that while the girl is asleep one morning, and her maid has time to watch over her, she in turn will have time to pick up her favourite cloche, which is being mended at the milliners. She calculates the trip should take half an hour on foot, that she will be back before her daughter wakes up. It is crucial that Sarah is with her as often as possible, as she is prone to violent fits. Sarah, frustrated by the way in which her life has narrowed over the past seven years, is unable to shake the guilt she feels at her own dissatisfaction with her child.

Mrs. Lifelong, the milliner, has passed the hat on to a trainee, a young girl who was due in the day before with the finished item, but who has not appeared and will, she assures Sarah, duly be sacked. Sarah, who has so far displayed faint signs of psychological uneasiness – reacting with puzzlement to the sound of her pennies dropping on the floor at the sweetshop counter – demands the girl's address, takes a cab to her flat.

After various comical revelations, by which it transpires that Sarah must follow the girl and the cloche across half of London, into the depths of Spitalfields, she arrives on Fournier Street at the door of a man who, she has been told, is the descendant of a Huguenot merchant. Here, the commotion of the busy alleyways fades. Nobody answers when she presses the bell. She turns the handle and enters.

Inside, bewilderingly intricate patterns accost her, exotic rugs hang end-to-end on the walls, carpet the floor. A small man with a smooth, almost featureless face, leads her through bright corridors to a large drawing room, where an open fire blazes, beside which the merchant and the young girl are sitting, rapt in eager conversation. Wrought with anxiety now – she has abandoned her child for many hours, and has developed an obsessive desire to lay her hands on the hat – she takes a step forward, and they stop talking.

After drinking a nacreous, sweet-smelling tea, Mrs. Morgan leans back into the sofa she is sitting on and falls into a trance-like state. She is immersed in memories of her childhood, at boarding school at a young age, in which phantasmagoric versions of children she had known, who had subjected her to terrible bullying, exaggerate the dark arts of their original selves:

Dressed in white, emerging and receding from the light of stolen candles, each girl seemed interchangeable. Sarah struggled to make out the faces she knew by name, her spare blouse pulled between her teeth, ears ringing still from an unseen blow to her head.

B.C.

The nightmare ends when she is made to sit in front of a mirror and cut her hand once for each girl, with a pair of sewing scissors, to mingle her blood with theirs, to prove her affection for them.

Sands was rising to his feet, scanning his bookshelves. He began to tell what Dad described later as a 'tall tale'.

I was sent from the room.

I shivered in the hallway, didn't try to listen at the door.

'There is something here that needs to be addressed,' said Sands, as Dad let me back in. 'There is the question of her mental stability. The question of potential physical abuse in the family cannot be avoided.'

'Do you want my permission to write about it?'

Sands paused. His face communicated a tortured sense of conflicting responsibilities.

'Because she never mentioned anything like it,' said Dad. 'And unless she comes back from beyond the grave, you won't know the truth, will you?'

Sands ran his tongue along the inside of his cheek.

'Perhaps not,' he said.

I now feel able to read the expression my father wore. It was a tacit apology.

As we got up to leave, Sands panicked. He begged us to stay. Dad looked him in the eye, told him not to worry, that nobody had been offended.

'What you have recounted may have happened that way.'

Sands turned to a drawer, took out a photograph.

'You should have this. It looks like proof to me.'

Dad thanked him, took it without looking at it, put it in his inside coat pocket. Sands watched us leave.

'He gave away the evidence,' I said.

'He's got a copy,' said my Dad.

My father and I never spoke about the meeting again.

'Let's go away together,' said Imogen. 'It's not like either of us is short on time.'

We were back in my flat.

'What about your work?'

'I need a break. You could do with one too, Issy.'

'You're always busy.'

'All the more reason.'

'I'll think about it.'

'You're not worried about me calling the other night?'

'You can remember it?'

'I was exhausted. I worked at the Maughan all day, then walked home to Belsize Park. You walk somewhere in London, apparently it takes a long time.'

'Where did you say you were walking from?'

'The library on Chancery Lane.'

She was lying now.

'That's a long way.'

'But you get to see the city. London's more beautiful than people give it credit for. I made a detour to Primrose Hill. Did you ever see 'Blow Up'?'

'Sure.'

'That's where they found the dead body. I always hope I'll see one there. Is that wrong?'

She giggled.

'Sure it is,' I said.

'Every time I get to the top I think, of all the places I've been to, London may well be the most beautiful.' She lay back, resting her legs on the arm of the sofa. 'Next time I go away, I'm taking you.' She sat up. 'Soon. Next week.'

'Not next week.'

'Why not? You can afford it.'

'That's got nothing to do with it.'

'If I had the money you had, I'd go away every other week. I'd buy a flat in Paris and New York. And a house in Geneva.'

'My parents were writers, not oligarchs.'

'They might as well have been cobblers, at this rate.'

She lay back down and shut her eyes. I went into the kitchen. I needed to take myself out of the room.

Imogen called through to me.

'Your problem is you're too suspicious. Of me, and yourself. I wonder what would happen if you were to have a good time?'

I walked back to the door.

'A good time?'

'Never mind.'

'A lot of what you say doesn't add up. For example, where is all this work you're doing? You haven't shown any of it to me. At the end of the day, how do I know you're not just another Marianne Sykes obsessive, getting kicks from spending time with her daughter?'

Imogen sat up.

'Isabel,' she said.

'I've told you everything about myself. I told you about the time my mother tried to kill herself in a swimming pool. You don't think I trust you?' My voice was rising. It had been a long time since I fired my thoughts out like this. 'What more do you want?'

'Calm down.' Imogen folded her arms. 'You're being paranoid.'

'I've every reason to be.'

She nodded. Then she reached for her bag. When she gave me the papers, my vision was blurred. Marianne Sykes: Inward Sight. The first paragraph was brilliant. Concise and original in style.

'You never asked me about it,' she said. 'I was beginning to be offended. Not that you're capable of being offensive.' She pouted mischievously, took my hand. 'And you're doubly forgetful. You never told me that about your mother.'

'The empty pool, in Florence.'

'You must have thought you did.'

I told her that I thought I was beginning to lose the plot.

Every nuance of emotion I had felt over the last few weeks seemed to have amassed, to demand expulsion. I told her that I could not sleep properly, that my days were spent in a kind of dizzy paralysis.

'Tell me about it now.'

I told her what had happened in the garden in Florence, that I had been too confused to cry afterwards.

'Well, now you know why I'm here.'

Imogen grinned.

'Why's that?'

'This stuff needs to come out. You're too shy to see a therapist.'

'Am I really so shy?'

'Yes.'

I told Imogen I could remember a time when she had pulled me up from the street outside my house, after I grazed my knee. Some time ago, the memory had returned to me.

It began with a deep red smudge on the tarmac and a sense of heat all around. She pulled me up, lifted my arm over my head, and I whirled away behind the trees. 'Isabel! We have to get home,' I think she called. I hid in some bushes. Her face emerged, tiny and distant, spied through broken leaves.

It was the first time I had told her I remembered her. She shut her eyes and frowned as though concentrating hard. At first I thought she might cry, but there were no tears. I thought of her reaching the peak of the tower in Sardinia again. She looked beautiful sitting there, her face tensed in that way, delineated by creases in skin that was usually flawless.

I reached for her shoulder, but she held her hand up, laughed.

'Need – space –' she pretended to gasp. I laughed too. 'I'm

not sleeping well either, remember! Someone keeps calling me!'

I took our cups through to the kitchen.

'You said that Jenny was coming down next week?' she called out. 'Well, if you're not up for a holiday, why don't we all do something together. Have a fun night. You could use it.'

I went back into the sitting room. She looked calm.

'I'm sorry Imogen.'

'I'm sorry too.'

The next day I walked into a café off High Street Kensington and saw Imogen. She was sitting with the two children I had seen her holding hands with, the day I followed her through the side streets, south of the Fulham Road. She saw me immediately, there was no escape. Her companions stared at me warily as I approached. The boy wore his hair in an immaculate side-parting, a stiff white shirt collar cuffed his neck. He looked away when I smiled at him. The girl's hair was pushed back by a black headband, her hands folded neatly on the table. Imogen took a slow sip of coffee, before her face brightened.

'Hello! Guys, meet my good friend, Issy.'

The children weren't convinced.

Imogen made a fuss over me, but I had already seen her expression when I walked in, something like suppressed anger. Now she seemed to be trying to impress the boy and the girl.

'I'm Isabel,' I said, holding my hand out to the boy.

He shook it. I couldn't catch the girl's eye.

'Sam and Kate,' said Imogen. She came to stand beside me. 'They really need my undivided attention,' she whispered.

'Whose are they?'

'They're mine,' she said. 'I'm joking.'

I rolled my eyes.

'Okay, Issy's going now!' said Imogen.
The boy nodded, so I left.

Brompton Cemetery joins Old Brompton Road to the western end of the Fulham Road, its paths turning through roughly cut grass, among London plane and yew trees, deodar cedars and the Japanese cherry. Dismembered figures of grey stone lean precariously over graves, telepathising. That winter, I would often sit there with a coffee and a cigarette, the city hidden, the traffic hushed, imagine myself in an abandoned, frost-locked province of some latter-day Arcadia.

I had arranged to meet Jenny at the main gate. She grinned and hugged me.

'This where you come to think of Mum?'

The thought hadn't occurred to me.

We chatted as we walked up the central path. Jenny laughed non-stop. The music in her voice was a stimulant. I glanced at her as she rocketed through the story of her weekend. She was a few inches shorter than me. When she turned towards me, her ice-blue eyes found me instantly.

We stopped by the domed Chapel, watched the sun draw a white blind over my bedroom window. She asked if it had felt strange, moving back to London.

We talked about the first time Dad drove us to the new house near Tidington in Oxfordshire. We had been staying with our uncle in Reading. I still remembered the landscape gathering and falling away on either side of the car, the lightbox of a forest's flashing interior, the purple gauze that slid across the far hills as evening arrived, stepping out into the dry heat that followed us up from the city. The smell of trees and unnameable flowers. Softness underfoot. The house in the darkness. Dream-house.

Jenny had found an enormous moth on the front door, bark

lines carved into its wings. A tiny contraption built from forest material. Dad blew on it and it vanished.

Jenny could not sleep that night, swore she could hear moths squeaking. Dad said that he had never heard moths making noises, but Jenny was convinced. We all stayed up, sitting round Jenny's bed, holding our breath. Just arrived from the city, learning to accept the silence.

Eventually, we agreed that moths could squeak.

We named the place Summer House. Dad ran through the things we could do the following day, now we were in the countryside. We could play rounders in the garden. We could go for a long walk. We could have a barbecue. He spoke quickly, then he disappeared into the depths of the building, forgetting to tell us where to find him.

Jenny and I sat on the steps of a curving colonnade. Withdrawn at school, she seemed to have collided with herself at university. Her skin was flushed and she talked excitedly.

'Remember designing our rooms?'

We each had our own in the new house. I had mine painted midnight blue. Jenny lined her walls with exquisite drawings in crayon, of the five of us, the four, the three of us children, just Jenny. 'A fine colourist,' Dad said, turning on the spot.

He had given us all a set of clear perspex boxes, which we filled with discoveries from the garden and the wood that encircled it: strange-shaped twigs, weird leaves, rocks like faces. We each had another box lined with blue velvet, which held something that had belonged to our mother. Mine contained a pearl necklace. Jenny had a silk scarf, enfolding a flock of Japanese cranes. We never knew the contents of Jonny's. The items kept by my sister and I were returned to the family by a friend who had borrowed them, changed by their owner's death into treasure, still smelling faintly of an unfamiliar perfume.

I never thought to ask Dad whether he kept one thing in particular himself. Perhaps the copies of my mother's works in

Italian translations, which filled a small shelf in his bedroom, were all that he wanted.

The quiet of the nights was amplified by the insect chatter wafting into our rooms that summer. Instead of the loud, often fraught, conversations downstairs, that had so often sent us to sleep before, the sound of pots and pans clanging together in the sink marked the end of the day now, finally petering out, tumbling music to accompany or invoke dreams. Some nights, dreams would agonise my body, flames forming on my skin, the bed damp with sweat when I awoke. I stopped calling out in the new place. Dad's room seemed to be further removed here, although it was only two doors away.

Jenny looked out across the graveyard. Her hair was gossamer thin, lifting in the breeze. I followed the sky blue veins on the bridges of her feet, running to the edges of her black pumps. Her hands were carefully cupped in her lap. I tried to trace the little girl's nape beneath her shifting hair, that delicate curvature I still held in my mind.

'You look tired,' she said. 'You keep going quiet.'

'I had a late night.'

'Graveyards,' she said, 'kill the mood every time.'

I had heard hints from Dad that she was hanging around with a bad crowd at Bristol, that she arrived home at the end of one term with dilated pupils and a short attention span. I had tried to explain to him that I did not think this was the end of the world. If she took drugs on the odd occasion, at least she kept getting her work done. But one of the few times she had called me, since starting university two years ago, was late at night, to let me know Dad was 'blanking her' at home. She was upset. I could tell she had taken something. I did my best to comfort her.

The guilt I felt at not having followed the call up returned for a moment, at not having called her much at all.

I realised that Jenny had not spoken for a while. Perhaps

we wouldn't make it through the day after all. The feeling of exhaustion returned.

I needed Imogen's help.

'I've got a surprise for you,' I said.

'I envy you.'

'Really?'

'You're completely free. To do whatever you want.'

'I don't know what I want.'

The pressure on the back of my eyes returned.

She looked at me directly.

'Yes, you do.'

For a moment, I almost believed her.

When Imogen arrived that evening, Jenny was asleep on the sofa. Imogen shook her head.

'She always used to sleep in that position.'

I decided not to ask her about the children I had seen her with in the café, to wait and see if she brought the subject up herself. Our reconciliation, beginning with her presentation of the essay on my mother's work, had become an unspoken pact, an invitation for me to trust her that could not be denied, however many unanswered questions I might still have. Imogen cast a long shadow, which became a cloak she slipped into each time we parted. A place she could be safe. I needed her to trust she could emerge from that place when she saw me again.

'Imogen!' Jenny recognised her instantly, sat up, astonished, blinking in the bright light.

For a moment I thought Imogen was going to hug my sister. She was transformed by a look of childlike delight. I felt a jab of envy.

Imogen regained her composure, directing the conversation. She and Jenny were soon running through countless memories they had of the times they had spent together. Many of them involved me, but I met their expectant glances, when called upon to contribute, with a shake of the head, reached for my cigarettes. Clearly my memory had been working to a different rhythm. I sat back and watched them talk, a little bewildered.

It was obvious that Imogen had played an important part in Jenny's life. Neither could remember how long she had worked for our parents, but the depth of the impressions she had left on my sister could not be questioned. Simply seeing and hearing Imogen seemed to leave Jenny transported.

Imogen caught my attention when I heard her describing something familiar to Jenny.

It was the sight of us filing out of the house with Jonny and Dad, up to the car on a weekday morning, ready for the school run. She remembered the scene remarkably well: the colours of our school uniforms, the way Jenny skipped around the car sometimes, arguments over the front seat. Jenny gave her a round of applause, said she remembered Imogen waving at us, on her way to her own school. And Imogen told Jenny of a state of mind that would often overtake her, which she had disclosed to me before, with the same quiet fervour. Passing our house, eyeing the windows, wondering what was taking place in the mind of Marianne Sykes.

Lying awake in bed and trying to think as this writer might.

'I wasn't old enough to think of her that way while she was alive,' said Jenny. 'You worshipped her.'

'You must have felt the glow that came from that creative energy, even if you didn't realise it at the time,' Imogen replied.

Jenny laughed.

'You've lost me,' she said.

'It's a certain radiance you can feel when someone is – ' She smiled, shook her head. 'Not everyone gets that kind of thing.'

'How were you going to finish?' I said.

'I'm sorry,' said Jenny. 'Tell us what you meant.'

Imogen smiled again.

We sat in silence for a while. The blinds were still up,

a reflection of the room hung over the street. At once, we realised we were staring at ourselves.

'I read once that ghosts can't see their own reflections,' said Jenny.

'Are you drunk?' I said.

'A little bit.'

'You're thinking of vampires.'

Imogen looked at Jenny.

'I'm always up for telling ghost stories,' she said.

Jenny nodded vigorously.

'Really?' I said. 'That's for late at night.'

'It's half-twelve,' said Imogen.

'We haven't even eaten yet,' said Jenny.

'No wonder you're so drunk,' said Imogen.

Jenny laughed.

'I'm starting to fade a bit,' I said.

'No excuses!' said Imogen. 'Who's up for it?'

'Yes!' said Jenny.

'I'm not starting,' I said.

'I'll start,' said Jenny. She thought for a moment. 'I'm stuck.'

A thought occurred to me.

'Do you remember the time when you said you saw Mum in the garden?' I said.

'I remember you telling me I'd imagined it.'

'You were shaking. You said she was waving.'

'A real ghost story,' said Imogen. 'Can you remember her expression?'

'No, but I felt something, she wanted something.'

'To tell you something,' said Imogen.

'Well, I really meant – '

Imogen tapped my shoulder.

'Your turn. Have you ever seen your mother's ghost?'

'All the time. In my memory.'

Imogen shrugged.

'Isabel doesn't want to play.'

Jenny frowned.

'Go on, Isabel,' she said. 'This is important.'

'How is it?' I said.

'We've barely talked about Mum.'

I was caught off-guard.

'We will. From now on,' I said.

I looked at Imogen.

'Not so silly after all,' she said.

I decided that I would give them something that would put this game into perspective. I poured myself another glass of wine.

I told them that I often thought about the view that Jonny and I had of my mother's face when it appeared in the mirror we had held up to watch the house burn, in our back garden in Hampstead. That we had held up the mirror so that we could tell when we needed to get help, that Jonny had felt that we would not be blamed for what was happening once the fire was out of control. That this no longer seemed to make sense, that it was difficult to remember nonsensical decisions with any peace of mind, made in such circumstances. That I had felt weightless when I saw my mother's face in the glass we were looking through, that she seemed to assume that weightlessness, gliding behind the windows of her bedroom, in a place where she should not be, doing something that she should not be doing, calmly and carefully inspecting an earring, lifting the diamond to her ear. I could find any number of visual details in which to drown myself: her emerald dress, kohl-black eyelashes, even the gossamer texture of her hazel irises, though I was too far away to have seen them that night. I began to feel good as I talked, pleased that I was able to articulate all of this, pleased by their silence. My mother dropping out of sight as black smoke slid into the bedroom, inking in the window. Get help, Jonny shouted, running ahead of me around the side of the house, into a gathering crowd, an awful crowd of my mother, dresses shifting, brooches glittering, faces lighting up, becoming strangers, crying out. The party had appeared outside our house.

Dad will be here, I thought. He was at the back, restrained by three men, who began to point when they saw us. Jenny was sitting on the boot of a car, wrapped in a trench coat, sucking her thumb.

'How's that?'

'Well told,' Imogen said quietly.

'We've never talked about this,' said Jenny, shaking her head.

'Good we got onto it,' said Imogen. She was nodding slowly. 'Jenny.'

'What?'

'Would you feel comfortable telling your side of the story?'

I looked at Jenny. She had seen a child therapist a couple of hours a week for a year after the house fire. Jonny and I were forbidden by our father to raise the subject with her. I watched Jenny tuck her legs under herself, her face hardening. If she had been tipsy just moments ago, she wasn't anymore. Before I had time to ready myself, she was talking.

'I remember reading in my room. You were outside.'

Imogen had asked the question, but Jenny addressed herself to me.

'I had heard there was no babysitter coming. I spent most of the evening watching you both through the window.'

She shifted her weight from one leg to the other, eyes lowered, hands on her lap, the muscles of her arms relaxed. A strong undercolour fired her pale skin. She spoke carefully, at a steady pace.

'I read my book for a while. Then heard footsteps on the staircase out the front. I went downstairs, heard the jingle of keys. I ran into the kitchen, hid under the table. The sound of heels in the hall told me it was Mum. I heard her humming. The sounds that she made seemed forced, like she was trying to calm herself down. She sounded strange. I didn't want to come out. She obviously thought we were all outside. I heard her moving pots and pans. "Camomile tea," she said. "Brewed properly." Saying the words slowly. Then she said, "The kids are in the garden," in a sing-song voice. She began to hum, peacefully. I could see feet in high heels. Gold buckles shining as she moved around the kitchen. I thought she was looking for the tin with the camomile inside. I stopped feeling scared about getting caught. I could hear the water bubbling on the stove. Maybe she's not going out, after all, I thought. I had found it hard to believe she would leave us on our own. Then she said, "Not for all the jewels in Asia." She was laughing. "Nor the diamonds in Africa." I heard her sweep the sideboard with her hand, matches falling across the floor. She took her shoes off, locked the back door. Then she left the room. I heard her going upstairs. I felt embarrassed and confused, so I stayed where I was. Soon I smelled something burning. The room seemed to be getting milky. It was too hot. I ran to the kitchen door and reached for the key, but I couldn't turn it, then to the window in the other room, and banged on it, but you didn't hear. You looked up, but I couldn't make you understand. So I went up to get Mum. Her door was locked, she was singing to herself. I was hitting my palm against the wood. She stopped and said, "I thought you were going to be grown up today, Jenny? Go and see your brother and sister in the garden. Look, they're having so much fun! Let's not worry, let's pretend I never came back. Then you get maximum brownie points. Mum's in a rush." I ran downstairs through a load of smoke, holding my breath, opened the front door and reached the street. I told a young couple, dressed for the party, what was happening, and they called the fire brigade.'

We sat in silence for a long time. I wanted to tell her to keep going. I felt I could hear the sound of the door shutting on the house, on what had happened, the magical access closed.

The smoke had seemed unreal to me, covering the bedroom window. But Jenny had run through the same smoke our mother breathed. Did that bring them closer?

'I have,' Imogen was speaking slowly, 'to tell you something. Both of you.'

She was looking at her hands, spoke as though announcing a decision, something settled on.

'Marianne Sykes has always been a great hero of mine. And I love and respect both of you. Which is what makes this difficult to say.'

Jenny was staring at her.

'You were never really meant to be alone that night. Your Dad called me up to ask if I would come and check on you. Your mother thought you'd be fine, wanted Jonny to take charge. But your Dad couldn't resist. "Just go round for a couple of hours," he said. "I'll tell Marianne about it tomorrow." So I was to come at ten, leaving just before midnight, when your parents got back.'

'But you had stopped coming to look after us by that point,' said Jenny.

'That's right. I stopped coming to look after you some time before. But I lived nearby, and your father just wanted someone to drop by. He knew the secrecy about the agreement wouldn't sound weird to me. I knew your mother well enough. I agreed.' She lit a cigarette, breathed the smoke slowly. 'That's when we should have been reunited, so to speak. But as I was walking along your street, I ran into your Marianne. She seemed unsteady on her feet. She asked me what I was doing, where I was going. She figured out that I'd been dispatched to your house. I said I was on my way to drop in, to see how everyone was doing. She said her children were her own business, and as I could see, she was about to check on them herself. I apologised, said that she was quite right. I wanted to sound polite, but I also wanted her to think I was playing along with her, so as not to land your Dad in it. She was swaying slightly as we spoke, in time with the music playing faintly at the end of the road. "I also forgot my earrings," she said. She smiled and shrugged. I said that earrings were an important matter. She looked at me suspiciously. "I've just heard that sarcastic tone from my husband." She said she had just been accused of being capable of leaving a party to collect her earrings, but not to check on her children. "What do you think about that?" She looked at me. Her eyes were locked on mine, even while her body swayed. She was magnetic in her green dress, there was something majestic about her, in her posture and governance, something imperious, despite the fact she was clearly a drunk.' Imogen lit another cigarette. 'Looking back on it', she said, 'it's as though the fire was burning already, in her dress, in the crazy blue at the edge of the sky that evening. I didn't notice it then, but now I see the flames flickering around the edges of her eyes.' She tapped the cigarette over the ashtray, scattering white flecks, slid her little finger across the tabletop, slipping the tray under the edge of the surface to catch the debris. 'She told me to go with her to the house, that she would put her earrings on and make camomile tea – gave me a wink, it was a strange kind of intimacy, an admission that she was drunk – and that I could check on the children. "Then we will both be fulfilling our roles," she said. I followed her to your front door.'

'Wait a minute,' I said. 'Jenny, you only saw Mum at home?'
Jenny nodded.

'Well, I waited just inside the hallway, unsure what I should do. I heard her muttering to herself, turning the hobs of the stove on. She passed me on her way upstairs, said the kids were in the garden, I should go and see them, round the side of the house as the back door was locked. But I thought that first I'd check the stove, since she had seemed so unsteady. I peered around the kitchen door. Two of the hobs were turned up high. A saucepan was bubbling over one of them. The scarf she had been wearing burned on the other. I left through the front door immediately, called the fire brigade on my phone. I should have just turned off the gas, covered the scarf with a wet tea towel. I panicked.' She crushed her cigarette butt in the ashtray. 'I'm sorry.' She shut her eyes. 'You could say it's all my fault.'

Jenny was shaking her head.

'I was sober,' said Imogen. 'I wasn't thinking clearly. I should have called your Dad after I'd first spoken to her. But your mother terrified me. And how was I to know what would happen?'

Jenny seemed to be staring at something distant, indistinct. Tears began to flow down Imogen's cheeks.

'Say something,' she said.

Jenny kept rocking her head back and forth, wearing the same absent expression.

'You weren't there,' she said.

'Why doesn't she believe me?'

Imogen put her hands to her face.

'She doesn't know what to think,' I said.

Imogen looked at me through her fingers, mascara-smeared. Those interminable blue eyes.

'I killed her.'

With two steps, Jenny lunged. I caught her arm before her open palm made contact with Imogen's face. Imogen grabbed her bag and left the flat.

A couple of nights later, I received a phone call from Nathalie, an old friend from university. I had not seen her for months. She was shouting over music.

'I'm at a party off Cheyne Walk. Your sister's here. She's not looking good.'

Jenny had gone to the pub to see some friends earlier that evening. It was her last night in London. I took the address, left the flat.

Outside the entrance to the building, I pushed the doorbell repeatedly. The intercom rattled and tinny music broke out. 'Second floor,' someone called.

The door was ajar, rattling under heavy bass. I pushed through a mass of people, a wall of warm, moist air, stepped over a girl in a cocktail dress, asleep, her red hair fanning out across the carpet. I found Nathalie, sitting on the edge of a marble bath, smoke drifting out the corner of her mouth, head lilting, gazing at my sister. With her free hand, she curled a strand of brown hair round her forefinger.

'Ah-ha,' she said, without looking round.

Milky water filled the bath. Jenny's head was propped above the surface, eyes closed.

'Get her out,' I said.

Nathalie stood up slowly. We lifted her onto the bathmat.

'I was keeping her warm,' said Nathalie.

I felt unable to assimilate what I was seeing.

'Did you run the bath?'

'No.'

I dried Jenny quickly, wrapped her in a bathrobe, switched a hair-dryer on, gave it to Nathalie.

'Sort her hair out.' Then I called an ambulance, locked the door. I knelt down, rested Jenny's head between my knees.

'What happened?'

Nathalie said that Jenny had been talking to another girl, that they had disappeared into the bathroom.

'This was how we found her. The table by the bath was covered in coke.' We looked at the table, which was clean. 'Gone,' she shrugged. 'She's breathing fine.'

'Who was the girl?'

Nathalie looked puzzled.

Jenny came to at the hospital, a short drive away. She said she remembered talking to Imogen. That they'd had a few lines together. That was it.

There was no danger of pneumonia, the doctor said. We took a cab the short way home. At two that morning, I put her in my bed, lay down on the sofa.

What was Imogen doing there? Was this her way of punishing me for not backing her up? Had she really been lying to us the other night? If so, why? She would give me an explanation, I decided finally.

A few hours later it began to get light. I checked on Jenny. She was breathing deeply. I wrote her a note and left for the Strand Campus of King's College. I needed Imogen's address, so I could catch her off-guard. The receptionist turned me away. She said that if I had Ms. Taylor's number – which I tried to use as proof that I knew her – then I had more than she could give me.

I hailed a taxi, asked for the north end of the street on which I used to live. It would be the first time I had returned there. Imogen had never told me the name of her road, but had described the walk to my house many times. I planned to follow her directions in reverse. I stepped out of the cab, glanced quickly round the tree-lined avenue that seemed somehow more sparse in colour and clutter than I remembered it, neater in the late morning light. Perhaps I was comparing it to memories of the view from summer months, when the trees formed a canopy of green over the road, the cars end-to-end by late evening. I knew I would not follow the familiar curve to my left, to look for the house that had inevitably replaced mine. I felt a sudden sense of irritation, to think that these were the circumstances in which I was returning. Imogen's behaviour had delivered me here, though I had planned to make it a happy occasion. I had sensed a fury would possess me, to give me the stomach to confront her at the crucial moment. But I hadn't expected the dizzying feeling that had started to surge in my head.

'I killed her.'

'You weren't there.'

What would I say when she opened the door?

I went the other way, past the library on the right. A neon playground stood at the corner of the next intersection on the left, empty now, fresh paint gleaming, a swing stirring in the breeze. I took the following right, Fawcett Road. The quiet of the streets quickened my nerves. It was as though the neighbourhood, which had formed the limits of my childhood world, had been cleared of its residents and retouched for the purpose of my private mission. The tarmac on some streets was newly laid, and had I rested my hand on the bark of the nearest tree, I would not have been surprised to find my palm imprinted with wet, brown paint.

Finally I came to a great oak tree, looming from a grassy bank, its hidden roots rippling the pavement. Imogen's house was on the road branching off to the left. I realised that I should not be looking for the massive, detached building I had worked on in my imagination. The terraced houses continued here, disappeared around a bend in the road. I felt light-headed, sat down on the bank, short of breath.

Perhaps I would open my mouth, and finally nothing would come out. Our friendship, barely tethered to the usual rules, seemed now, as I lay back on the grass, the insides of my eyelids glowing orange in the sunlight, like a helium balloon floating steeply out of reach. Jenny, I hope you're okay, I said to myself, touching my phone in my pocket. I'll call you when I'm done. I breathed in deeply, exhaled, set off along Grass Hill Walk. I knew I was looking for a house called something-Court. It did not seem to be the right kind of road for a house with such a name. The ones I passed were numbered only.

I came to another intersection. Past this, the road continued, and the houses were small, semi-detached, dilapidated. Three rusted bicycles lay strewn across the nearest lawn, long grass shooting through the spokes of the wheels. The paintwork on the doors, around the windows, was dull and chipped. A rotary washing line turned in the breeze further up, creaking gently. I followed the street until it turned into a dead end, a red-brick wall, up against which reams of rubbish had blown. I could not think where I might have taken a wrong turn.

I returned to the intersection at the start of this part of the street, stopped, looked back. The clouds had begun to power across the sky, long shadows gliding over all I could see. There was nobody around to ask about the Taylor family. The wind grew stronger.

I felt as though Imogen was watching me.

As I turned to leave, I caught sight of a street sign. The name of this part of the road was not Grass Hill Walk. It was Garden Court.

I walked as fast as I could to the tube station, headed for South Kensington. There was one more place she could be. I asked myself again why she had kept it secret. By the time I had wound through the side streets, found the long, empty road with the high walls, I felt as though my nerves would overwhelm me. Outside the door I had seen her emerge from, I pressed the bell on the intercom, waited for the inevitable response.

'Hello?'

It was the voice of a middle-aged woman.

'I'm here to see Imogen.'

'Who is this?'

'Isabel Sykes. Imogen is the nanny.'
Silence. The voice clicked off.

.

When I got home, Jenny announced that she had called Dad. He was working on a book in Rome. He asked her to join him for a few weeks, said that he would speak to someone at her university. We stood on the steps outside my building that evening, waiting for her taxi to Heathrow. I asked her again if she remembered what had happened at Nathalie's. She shook her head.

'Will you speak to Dad about it?'

She looked away.

'I couldn't find Imogen,' I said.

'It doesn't matter.'

'You were furious with her. What about the story she told us? Could she've been right?'

Jenny looked at me wearily. We stared at the end of the street.

'I remember one thing from the party. She asked me to stay away from you.'

'What?'

'She said that you were in a bad way.'

'Me? We've got one basket case and someone in hospital, and I'm in bad shape?' I said.

'Dad's worried about you. He asked me to visit you.'

I said nothing.

'Imogen has spoken to him. She said you needed a break from your family. Less pressure,' said Jenny.

'He hasn't stopped delegating.'

'I've tried to get through to you, but you don't listen.'

'You can talk to me.'

'We need you.'

'You need to learn to help yourself.'

'You're not even warm yet.'

Her cab arrived.

That night, I ran through the clearest convictions I had about Imogen. I believed she was a student at King's. Her passion for my mother and her work was genuine. I knew she had some kind of relationship with the two children in Chelsea. She was probably their nanny.

What about Garden Court? What about the party? What about the last night at my flat?

Not only had she claimed to know my mother killed herself, she had wanted to take responsibility.

Why would she make this up? And now, did she think she could just vanish?

The fear that had engulfed me at the end of Garden Court returned. Like a svelte cat entering through a small gap in a window, soon it seemed to fill the whole room. I felt a new and worrying sensation, a burning on the backs of my legs.

The dizziness came back in the early hours of the morning, pounding my body. I threw up in the bathroom, the night seemed to roll over me.

I need to get away from here, I thought. Get some sleep.

When I arrived at Summer House, it was early morning, the bark of the silver birches lining the driveway tinted blue, the trees of the forest still blacked-in behind. I got out the car, breathed the searing air, felt my eyes and ears sensitise. The sky was ultramarine, streaked by the dark undersides of clouds. I sensed the mass of the building, undefined against the flats of the shadows.

I found the key taped to the inside lintel of the coal shed. At the porch, I stopped, looked down the drive the way I had come.

Cast my mind back.

Three cars pulled up quietly. The interior lights came on, soundless conversations took place. Three girls alighted, carrying holdalls and sleeping bags, a parent behind each wheel. The girls drifted towards me. I turned to the door.

I was tired.

'Tired,' I said to myself, hearing the burr of an echo in the unlit hall. My body was charged with some arcane energy. I passed into the sitting room, stood still. The wind turned outside, the front door closed. I tried to calm my brain, but it ran hectic, there seemed to be no way to slow it, to turn it off.

Jenny had felt that I needed help. Imogen wanted to keep her away from me.

Rather than tapering to points that made sense, my thoughts seemed to fork, to variegate, to multiply beyond me. I wanted a cigarette, the taste of wine. I needed Imogen near me.

I saw Jenny's head propped above the opaque bath water, the skin of soap suds dispersed across the surface like lilies. Her eyelids seemed to have swelled and reddened, her hair was darkened by the water, smoothed back to her scalp and crown. I had been alone at home, unable to sleep. Why couldn't I? I closed my eyes, imagined myself in Jenny's position. I felt the lukewarm water, the helmet of wet hair pressing on my head. Screwed my eyes up. Would anybody hear me scream?

I made my way upstairs. My bedroom felt unfamiliar. The curtains were drawn, the air smelled of detergent. I lay down on the bed, swung towards, then back away from sleep.

My shoulders rolling. Legs passing over my head. All around was deep blue. I kicked beneath myself, woke gasping for breath.

The windows were dark still. I passed across the landing to the bathroom, splashed my face with water. My head was black with a dirty corona of grey, in the mirror above the sink, in the moonlight coming from the frosted window.

Gradually, a series of objects slipped into my head, seen under a darkening gauze. A kettle. A cafetière.

I could taste almonds, my breath smelled bitter. Had I got up at some point to drink coffee? Drifted off again, without fully waking?

I watched the drops of water sparkle across the bowl of the basin. The beginning of my somersaulting dream returned to me.

I was pushing through a party, across bright marble, through a galaxy of iridescent jewellery. The guests turned away from me. I was looking for someone. A waiter swayed past with a silver tray.

I took a glass of champagne, but the party was emptying. Found a woman with her face averted in the final room.

Dived into a lagoon.

Sitting on the edge of the bath one afternoon, I realised I was talking out loud. Nothing dramatic, an aid to memory, I thought as I caught myself. But the sentences had begun to sound like an incantation: eyes shut, I was running through the day of the house fire in my mind, recounting events as I remembered them, holding them in order, palms suspended in the air.

I opened my eyes, blinked under the yellow light, stared at my pale legs. They had grown thinner since I arrived.

I turned the taps on.

That day the rushes of panic had intensified. My mind had blanked whilst I was standing at the kitchen sink. A glass broke in my hand.

Miraculously, it collapsed in on itself and I wasn't cut.

Steam filled the room, and as I lay back in the water I found myself unable to resist the traction of a handful of memories.

My mother smiling under the trees at the foot of our garden, stippled by sunlight. Lying on the floor of the pool in Florence. Talking to me there, a short while before.

I remembered Jenny, standing in her bedroom doorway.

She was fully dressed. I was going to the bathroom to get a glass of water. It was the middle of the night.

I spoke to her softly. She did not react. In her early teens, Jenny had begun to sleepwalk.

She waved her arm in front of her slowly. It was not the wave of a greeting or a farewell. She was testing something in the air.

Dad had long since given up staying awake all night, supposedly ready to catch her at an open window, to guide her back from a busy road. It turned out her adventures were entirely harmless: she would turn a tap on and off a few times, kneel in a corner and count her fingers, smile beatifically, sitting on the laundry basket. He would lock the doors before bedtime, keep the key to her window by mutual agreement, and allow her the 'freedom of the night'.

'Don't wake her,' Dad said.

That night I approached. I remember stealing something

from her. I crept to her side, looked into her eyes for a few full seconds. She rarely made prolonged eye-contact with anyone. It felt wrong. I saw the grain of her irises, hazelnut and heather. But her soul was closed to me. I extracted nothing but a pang of guilt.

She stretched her arm out, sweeping slowly. I got out of her way.

I was standing in front of the cheval mirror in my bedroom one evening in London. I had heard my mother going downstairs. Slowly, I pulled off my clothes. The evening light suffused the room with greyish green, filtered through the blue curtains where stitched ships rocked in the breeze. I remember my expression in the mirror: brow strained, lips drawn. I forced my gaze across my body, small shoulders, shins and feet.

An argument. Someone had insulted me.

I remember my expression sliding, silently imploring my body to grow. Holding my palms up in the strange light, willing the days that ran to the future to collapse.

Got dressed and crept downstairs. The others were out. Mum was asleep on the sitting room sofa, fully stretched, her head and feet on the edge of the seat, the base of her spine pressed against the back. I watched her breathing deeply. Her cheek twitched. A book lay beside her on the floor, the pages fanned out, holding it upright. Her white shirt twisted underneath her, chest rising and falling. A car passed by outside, then silence. I put my shoulder to the edge of the sofa, pivoted myself up into the space outlined by her belly and thighs, tucked my legs in, chin on knees. Pretended to sleep.

I broke a vase in the villa in Florence. White shards of china skimmed outwards across the floor. I stood in silence in the empty sitting room, unable to calculate how long it would take me to gather the pieces before somebody came in and discovered what had happened.

My mother's voice.

'Don't move.'

I was standing barefoot on the parquet boards, trapped by the shards everywhere. She began to collect them, touching only the curved surfaces, dropping them into the largest. She left the room without speaking.

I stood on the spot, looking out the window as a white cloud inched across the sky. The bin was being emptied in the kitchen. I ran into my bedroom, jumped into the closet, pulled the doors closed behind me. One of them swung open slightly.

Closely followed by my mother.

'Isabel?'

She was out there for some time. Waiting.

I snapped upright in my room at Summer House. With the lucidity of wakefulness, I had slid out from my bed, as though on a gurney, drifted up to the ceiling. From there I could see myself sleeping. I had panicked, rushed to get back under the covers, felt my body judder.

The room glowed with a chord of morning light.

Hold it together.

Hold what together? What points of orientation?

My brain felt like the dust motes I could see whirling in the sunshine, that circled one another but would not join, dissecting all that was solid, each bright point of light dying at the close of a momentary life.

Fragmented images came to me.

An oval bar of white soap, tied with strands of dark hair.
My mother's hands, limp and blanched against an unlit doorway.
Flowers in a garden, stitched into dresses.
The glass breaking in my uncut palm.
Rational thought subverted.
Through the wormhole.
Short-term memory wiped.

I got up and went to Jonny's room, breathing deeply, lay down in his bed. The birds outside warned that I had not slept properly again.

On the edge of sleep, I thought I could hear my phone ringing.

The Snowfall

'Where are they?' I said.

My mother wrapped her hand around the end of the phone.

'They're on their way.'

'Where though?'

She put her finger to her lips.

'How did it go?' she said to my father. 'And the garden?'

I imagined a garden in the countryside. It was full of white statues of Greek gods.

'And the drive?'

She turned around, mouthed *snowing.*

'How close are they?' I whispered.

'The weather report said it's heading to London. It's following you back.'

I dashed to the window. It was getting dark. There was no sign of any snow outside.

I had missed the trip to look at new houses. 'We're not even sure we'll move,' my mother had said. And I had needed to see the dentist.

She put the phone down.

'How's your mouth, little one?'

'It's fine. How's your headache, Mum?'

'Gone now.'

I looked out the window.

'How far away are they?' I said. 'Is the snow thick?'

'Dad said they're in a blizzard. Your brother and sister are finding it difficult. You got the better end of the deal.'

My mother left the room.

The floor was scattered with books and pencils. I had been doing my geography homework, colouring a map of the world.

'Where else is it snowing?' I called out, heard drawers opening and closing in the kitchen.

'What?'

'In the world.'

I heard the heating come on, the soft ignition of the pilot light, looked at the glossy surface of the dining table, the golden veins in the wood beneath the lampshades. Lay down on the carpet, began to scribble with the worn ends of green and blue pencils. I tried to make the oceans swirl.

My mother came in, saw the picture.

'The blue should be flat,' she said. 'It's more of a diagram. Show the waves in a different picture,' she said.

I set about scribbling horizontal lines. After a few minutes, the pencil fell from my hand.

'I'm bored,' I said.

'So suddenly?'

She was sitting on the sofa now.

'Will they be okay?' I said.

'Your Dad's seen plenty of snow before.'

'Have you been to Russia?'

'No! I wish I had been, though.'

'What's the snow like there?'

'Deeper. Colder. More like sand.'

'Does it ever snow in Africa?'

'Maybe in some parts. On mountains.'

I picked up the map.

'Show me where.'

'I couldn't say exactly.'

'Oh.'

I sat back down.

'We're just here, really, aren't we?' I said.

'What was that?'

'Waiting for the snow.'

She nodded thoughtfully, sat on the sofa by the main window.

'I remember waiting for it to snow one time when I was your

age,' she said. 'I went to bed, and the town was white when I woke up.'

'I'm not going to bed.'

'I wouldn't dream of suggesting it. This was the Christmas holidays. We drove to a place called Eastnor Castle. It's about half an hour away from where we lived.'

'Had it snowed there?'

'The snow hushed everything: no one else was around. It was as white as flour, white as the fingers of a god. And everything else looked black against it. We walked through the grounds, into the woods and out. At times it seemed as though the land was dwindling into the sky. And so many greys, a spectrum of grey.'

'Which god?'

'A god who had only just been born. A great black swan landed on the edge of the frozen lake by the castle that morning. She needed to hide. But the white landscape would not let her. So she pushed herself through the snow until she was as white as the fields all around. She craned her neck, admiring her new image in the polished ice. Then she noticed a cloud bumbling past overhead. Unable to understand why, she found herself drawn towards it. It was whiter than snow. Up she flew, and away.'

'What was the swan hiding from?'

'Who knows? What matters is the ice cracked later that morning at the place where the swan landed, and a new god slipped out.'

'A god! Did you see him?'

'It's difficult to say. There might have been a moment when I might have done, though. Want to hear?'

'Yes.'

'We were walking through endless snow, my mother and father and I. Then we saw the frozen lake, like a jewel sunk into the landscape.'

'The same one the swan found?'

'Yes. I wanted to play on it. My parents said no. So I caused a fuss. I ran towards it. But I couldn't run very fast. The snow was deep.'

'How old were you?'

'I must have been your age, or thereabouts. My Dad easily caught up with me, but I dodged as he stretched out, heard him fall. I ran back into the woods, a flock of hidden birds shook the trees. I kept going. As I heard my parents' shouting dying away, I came across some footprints. They were as small as mine. I was puzzled, because the footprints seemed to begin mid-tack, out of nowhere. Undisturbed snow, then there they were. I decided to follow them. I ran alongside the footprints till my face became so cold I could hardly move it. Every now and then a rook would call out. I would stop, look up, see a rookery in the branches above. Spindly clusters like strange spider-webs. Homes for ghosts. Then I would run again.'

'Weren't you scared?'

'Maybe I started to get a bit scared now. I had to ask myself, what would I find when these footprints came to an end? Or worse, would I find anything at all? Might they not vanish again, into the snow? The fear of getting lost spurred me on. Then I had an idea. I stopped to examine the footprints. Do you know what I saw?'

I put my hands over my eyes.

'I saw that they were very similar to mine. I wanted to test their size. So I stepped into them. Then I felt myself running backwards a little, drifting into the wind. It was a very strange sensation. I became like a leaf, or so it felt, tipped gently that way and this. A rook made a noise overhead, and I realised that I was unable to see my hands or my legs. So what could I do? I had to keep drifting for a time. Soon I was lifted up, over the tops of the trees, able to see quite clearly out over the quilted countryside. And then I saw myself walking below.'

'No!'

'The funny thing was, down there, I was wearing red tights. Strawberry red. I don't remember ever having owned a pair like that. I saw myself disappear under some treetops. I floated down, willed myself beneath them. There was another lake, deep, murky red. A lake filled with blood.'

'No!'

I looked at my mother.

'You made it up,' I said.

'Look.'

She pulled up her trouser leg, showed me her ankle. A crescent scar appeared, pale and shining, when she turned her leg in the lamplight.

'This is where I nicked myself, running from my parents.'

'That's from the swimming pool,' I said.

'Ah, yes.' She pulled her trouser leg down. 'You know, I can't remember that happening any more. It must have been scary for you.' She looked at me. I felt embarrassed. It was the first time she had spoken about it. I was still not entirely sure what had happened back then. But I blamed her for my uncertainty.

'I promise to be more careful in future.'

'Take a torch, Dad said.'

'Take a torch. Then I won't get caught like a heffalump.'

'Heffalumps don't get caught.'

She patted my head.

'You were going to throw my dress away,' I said.

She frowned.

'Oh, no. I put it outside your room.'

'You took it.'

'I was in a bad mood. Parents get like that too.'

'Once Jenny took a bracelet from my chest of drawers and hid it. And you wouldn't let her come downstairs till she brought it down. And you made her say sorry.'

'I said sorry, didn't I?'

'I can't remember.'

'Don't look at me like that, Isabel! I'm sure I did.'

I picked up my pencils and exercise book, looked out the window.

'Where are they?' I said.

'On their way.'

'Is Dad driving?'

'I told you this, Isabel.'

I turned and flung the pencils at her.

'They could crash and you don't care!'

My mother looked shocked.

'Your father's a very good driver.'

'It's a blizzard! He can't see where he's going.'

'He'll be able to see the road.'

I began to scream. She tucked her legs up under her.

'Selfish!'

She looked at the floor.

'You're selfish!'

'Isabel.'

'You heard!'

'I don't know what you mean,' she said quietly.

'You're not my mother.'

'Isabel, I don't understand.'

'You're pretending.'

I raced upstairs, opened my wardrobe, pulled out the dress my father had bought for me in secret in Florence. Took it down to my mother.

'Take it back.'

I ripped it from the collar to the hem. She caught it as it sailed through the air, spread shapeless on her lap.

'That's a funny present,' she said distantly.

I ran at her and she grabbed my forearms. I could feel her muscles trembling.

'If I didn't say sorry, then I'll say sorry now. I'm sorry,' she whispered.

'You can't just say that.'

I began to cry, tried to jerk my body away.

'I mean it,' she said.

We were quiet for a while.

'There wasn't a lake of blood.'

'Sure was.'

'Really?'

'But only in the story.'

I felt my muscles begin to give way.

'I stopped myself from crying,' I said.

'Well done.'

'I ripped the dress.'

'You were very angry.'

'It's my dress,' I said.

'Was your dress.'

I giggled.

'Isabel, look at me.'

She put her hand to my face. She was crying.

'Don't cry,' I said. 'That's not fair.'

'I'm sorry.'

I ran up to my room.

Laid out on the floor were all the books I had needed to complete my homework that weekend. Sums, a picture of a section of the Bayeux Tapestry, a drawing of our house from the street and other sheets and notes covered the carpet. I kicked them all to one side, sat down in the middle of the floor. Pictured my father, brother and sister, saw them through the windscreen of the car, the wiper working back and forth in the midst of the tumbling snow. My father, eyes on the road ahead, concentrating steadily. I jumped up and shut the door.

I wanted them to be back. Instead, the house was silent and my mother was on her own downstairs. I began to hum loudly. I did not want to hear her crying. Dad, Jonny, Jenny in the car. Patient, like they were waiting to say something to me.

I wondered whether Dad would be angry when he got back, with Mum so upset. Perhaps she would come upstairs, to find me, to shout. I crawled under my bed. From here I could see across the room to the space beneath Jenny's bed, where more books, a toy radio and an old blue set of plastic cups and saucers were stacked. She would ignore me later, if I was in trouble. I lay still, humming quietly, till I lost my sense of how long I had been there.

The front door opened. No car sound. Slowly, I inched my way out into the brightness of the room, went to the window, ducked under the curtain, stood on tiptoe.

Snow drifted out of the darkness towards me.

I climbed onto the sill, resting on my knees, lifted the handle. The cold came into the room. It had been snowing for a long time. The houses surrounding ours were covered, the street seemed quieter than usual. A thickness of flakes appeared within the corona of each street light. I realised my face was hot.

My mother was carefully descending the steps. She stopped at the top of the drive, a smooth white rectangle now, which sloped gently down to the road, put her hands on her hips, looked at the sky. Then she disappeared round the side of the house, returned with a spade and began to shovel the snow, beginning at the near corner. With long, scraping strokes of the blade, she worked through strips of white, across and down, across and down, small piles building on either side until, halfway through the process, she stood up, put her hand to the small of her back.

I tensed. She had forgotten her torch again. She might fall.

She tested the black asphalt she stood on now with a sweep of her left foot. Then the shovelling continued, as the snow fell faster, surrounding her. I turned away, unable to watch and the light bulb swung into view, a blinding light that forced my eyes shut.

The Kitchen

Jenny began to scream when Dad pulled up to our Uncle's house. He hauled her over his shoulder, moved up the avenue of small trees that made a path to the porch. The lights were on inside, the garden was tangled in long shadows. I stopped beside the front lawn. It was covered in molehills, dark like holes in the grass.

Jonny hissed, and I followed them up the path.

Uncle Simon led me and my brother and sister into the sitting room, said he and my father would return in a moment.

'Look after your sister, guys.'

Jenny was still screaming. She was curled up on the sofa now, her face twisted, frozen like a baby's, a mask of shapeless emotion. Jonny covered his ears and scowled. I followed my uncle back into the corridor, through half-remembered passageways, crouched down before the door to the kitchen, which had been left ajar, and listened.

'You shouldn't be here,' said my uncle.

'Where should I be?'

'You'll be needed.'

'What happens? Nobody told me.'

'Did you speak to the police?'

'No. I made a run for it.'

'You'll be needed for something.'

'What about them?'

'I could've picked them up.'

'I have to go in there.'

Silence.

'I'm sorry,' my uncle said, finally.

'I came here for something to say to them.'

'You're in shock. But let that help you be practical, for now.'

'What did you say when Jessica died?'

'That's another story.'

'What's happened, Simon?'

I heard a whining in my father's voice. He sounded like a child.

'I don't know what's happened. Marianne's gone.' He paused. 'You can say anything for now.'

'She believed in heaven. I think.'

'That's a good place to start. Then you must go back to London. You can leave them here.'

'You've got work tomorrow.'

'Go.'

I heard my uncle leave by another door.

'Dad.'

The kitchen was half-lit. My father looked inhuman for a moment, then I realised his hands were covering his face.

'Dad.'

He didn't move.

'I'll go with you.'

He shook his head.

'No, Issy.'

'We have to go back to London.'

'No.'

'We can't keep her waiting.'

He lowered his hands slowly.

'She won't mind waiting, Isabel.'

Neither of us was sure what we meant.

He led me back to the sitting room, told us that our mother was dead. Jenny stopped crying then.

Uncle Simon came in, put the television on. Dad left for London.

I looked up. My brother and sister were wrapped in duvets on the other two sofas in the room. I had been unable to go to sleep completely. They had gone quickly, suddenly, falling as though touched by fairy dust.

I had a sense of my mother leaning over water, over deep, glossy shadows on a silvery surface, as though disinterested in the laws of gravity, neglecting to support herself by grasping a branch or a rope. The TV was off. I rubbed my eyes. The gentle rhythm of Jenny's breathing filled me with a sense of tranquillity. A certain knowledge forced itself upon me: my mother was going to meet me in the kitchen. She was not there yet, but when she was, I would know. I relaxed, let my body droop, lay back down. My head touched the pillow.

My mother was sitting on a chair in front of me, reading a book.

'I'll see you in the Kitchen,' I said.

She looked at her watch.

I heard a sound like running water, sat up in bed. The sound stopped. The house was quiet. I reached for the light. A gentle rustling outside. It was raining. I switched on the bedside lamp, switched it off again, listened to the gentle clamour at the window. The sound like running water returned. I sat up. Coming from downstairs. There was a subtle resonance, like a cloth-covered hammer hitting a pan. I crept over to the bedroom door, rested my fingers on the handle.

Another resonance. If it was a burglar, he would go. I just had to wait.

It sounded as though someone was playing an exhausted xylophone. I checked the clock by my bed: 2.20AM. Thought I heard a sound on the stairs. A glass smashed in the kitchen.

Where was my phone? I picked up my old hockey stick from its place by my wardrobe. It felt too light. Turned the door handle soundlessly, slipped out onto the landing.

I shouted.

'Get out!'

The noise continued.

I swung the stick a little. Could I use it? Hitting the back of someone's head, the hard reverberation in my hands. Was I allowed to hurt someone? I decided I didn't care. Then I imagined a knife going into my stomach, the alien metal inside me, sat down on the stairs.

The house was dark. The sound of the rain enclosed the place. The road felt far away. There would be no cars at this time, I reminded myself. If I had any sense, I would find somewhere to hide.

But I had already called out. If someone or something wanted to find me, they had all night. I gripped the wood tightly.

'The police are coming!'

Silence. Did burglars in the countryside carry knives?

'Dad! Jonny! Wake up!'

I didn't sound convincing. Jars rattled on the kitchen sideboard.

I should have stayed in my room, I thought. Now I have no choice. I can't just sit here. I stood up, felt the thud of blood in my ears, tried to place my feet gently at the base of each step. The floorboards stuck to my skin. Another glass shattering on tiles, louder. I sat back down. I'm staying here, I thought. My hands shook. I pushed the hockey stick down against my knees.

Ignoring the crashes of noise, I focused on the softer sounds that threaded them together. The rain confused them, but the lack of process, of logic underpinning them, made me think of a drunk or a child.

It struck me that I could not hear footsteps.

Could it hurt me if it didn't have feet?

I crept down to the hall, walked to the door of the kitchen, switched on the light.

A small bird wheeled into the window, tumbled over the sideboard, skimming the floor, landed beneath the table. I shook my head and grinned.

'This has to be a joke.'

I went back upstairs, got dressed, brought a bed sheet down from the airing cupboard. Remembering the broken glass, I put my trainers on. I opened the sheet in front of me, moved towards the table. The bird refused to appear. I stood still.

'We could be here all night.'

Something moving outside.

A fear that was greater, opening under and around the panic that clung to the edges of my mind. Whatever had drawn me downstairs in the first place, drew me to the front door. I pulled the latch. The night swung open before me, a wall of rain traced faintly by the kitchen light at the rear of the hall. I flicked the outside light switch. The drive stretched away into the trees. I felt a sudden pang for the bird's safety, trapped with all that broken glass.

I put my coat on, stepped out into the smell of wet grass and soil.

'Hello?'

The trees churned. My voice fell back on me. I followed the curve of the gravel. Turning back, I saw the porch light broken and scattered by leaves.

The door ajar, swinging gently.

'Hello?'

The knocking of branches.

My spine felt like an energy meter, winding slowly but surely downwards. No strength in my legs. The night had sucked them dry. The end of the drive turned and extinguished itself some way off. I tried to outstare the place it might have led to.

The only person out here was me.

I had dreamt up an intruder. A murderer for company. A killer to guard me against the night.

I turned back towards the house and saw the sitting room light on. I myself, or someone very like me, was watching from the window. Calmly, quietly, from deep inside.

Unconsciousness seemed to threaten me then, like a spider sliding down an invisible thread. I held my ground as the path swayed.

The figure stood still, slipped out of sight.

Two thoughts occurred at the same time.

You've gone mad. Imogen.

Inside the light in the hall was off now, as was the light in the sitting room. It took me a while to make her out.

She was sitting with her legs crossed, pulled up under her chin, naked in the centre of the floor.

Why are you doing this. If it's me who needs help, I said to myself.

'Time to go,' I commanded. 'Enough is enough.'

She didn't move. So I stumbled upstairs, my chest grazed by something like sorrow. Perhaps I understood that soon we'd have to part for good. Perhaps I understood that it wasn't sorrow. It was a stranger feeling, a swifter current, one that ran darkly through my fingers.

Footsteps. I turned my head on the pillow. Imogen was at the door to my room.

In the moonlight I could see she was still naked. Silent, as she was at the flat. As though it were a familiar routine, a ritual of ours.

Of course, it was, in a sense.

She came closer. Silence again. She had stopped moving. Then I felt the slow depression of the bed.

Stop now. Before it all comes undone.

I had made myself immobile. The ultraviolet smell of nail polish, strengthening.

Imogen lay down beside me, the milky plane of her back warm in front of me, the smell of herbs from her freshly shampooed hair, herbs I felt I could name but now they escaped me, herbs to mend and to poison, her hand on mine, lifting it now, bringing it round to her front and down across the night to her sex, the knot in the dark, the place where the night might finally claim me.

I felt myself scream, twist her hand back.

Imogen's naked body coiled in the moonlight, slipping to the floor.

It was a dream, perhaps.

I twisted harder.

She made no sound, but her body spasmed, as though commanded by the hand.

'What do you want?' I shouted. I realised I was crying.

It was as though I had reached a precipice, found a creature there who had to be made to give up her secret.

A noise, a sob, came in reply.

'What's wrong with you?' said Imogen quietly. 'I just want to be close to you.'

'Why?'

'I care about you. You're the one not making sense.'

'Who says I have to make sense?'

'Isabel, listen to yourself. You're heading for a fall. You don't know what you're doing anymore. Why are you out here by yourself?'

'To get away from you. To get away from questions like that.'

'The concerns of people who love you.'

'You don't love me. You're a freak.'

'Isabel!'

'A groupie. A hanger-on. A stalker.'

'I saw you watching me when I left the house that time. With the children. Who stalks who?'

She was trying to turn towards me, but her bent arm held her back, her face obscured by the shadow of her hair.

I laughed.

'The concerns of people who love me.' I struggled to discern her profile in the half-light. 'I suppose one of them is you?'

'You haven't slept for some time.'

'Is it any wonder when you keep coming into my room?'

'I'm your friend.'

'I never really trusted you.'

'That's not true.'

'Do I sound like I'm lying?'

'We shared special times together.'

'We never really connected. Friends connect.'

'How do they? If we don't connect with one another, who does? Look at us!'

'Look at us!'

'A connection is reading each other's thoughts in the dark. Stepping into each other's dreams.'

I hesitated.

'I don't like the sound of that.'

'You've dreamt about me, Isabel. I know you have. I could help you sleep, if you'd let me.'

'Why did you pretend to be responsible for my mother's death?'

Silence. I twisted her arm a third time. This time she cried out.

'What happened that night? I have to know, Imogen. The truth, now. No more stories.'

'I've tried to do you a service. What it was, you might never understand. But one day you'll thank me.'

'Do you even know?'

The final answer, the diamond shining in the night, diminishing, vanishing.

'You don't know yourself anymore,' said Imogen. 'I knew a very different girl, when she was a child. You'll be lost if you don't find her again soon.'

A very different girl.

Was I lost now, or at the height of my powers? Beyond rescue, or back in control?

Either way, I had acted. I let go of her hand. She crept away.

I was left with the dark, the sigh of the blind in the faint breeze the window let in, and a slice of pale stellar light above the windowsill, an image of my own soul drifting into deep space.

I stayed awake for a long time, listening. When I heard the front door open and shut, I went downstairs and turned the key.

I was unpractised in waking from deep sleep.

The appearance of consciousness, oxygen-laden after deep and cloudy waters, expansive like a field of yellow wheat lurching round the elbows, ripening, clarifying, mixing with sunlight, forceful, unbalancing, the smell of smoke on summer afternoons, a curious thing, not unwelcome, then a tiny ignition in the vast night beneath, from downstairs a finger of heat that prodded my skin. I tried to put the house together room by room, waking as I moved, aware of hot air pressure and a shaggy beast brushing the staircase. Swarm-hum. I began to inch down the steps to the front door. A moment's pause and I'd have been stuck. I had no desire to jump out of a window. A wall of red flame and black smoke moved on my right. I could have run my hand through it like a waterfall.

It progressed to the bottom of the stairs. Fire licked at me and seared my skin, whiplashed my elbow. *Stop dreaming.* I did not have time to watch myself on the stairs, with the steps higher up blackening now. I pictured myself panicking, unable to move. Death by a thousand thrashes. Tuck your feet under, take a long snooze. Or jump to the hallway floor. *Let's move.* The front door was locked but the key was in, where I'd left it. I stumbled under the fury of the burning building, out into the early light, away from the conflagration softened by falling rain, fed by midwinter breezes.

I began to cry. Great, shuddering bouts of emotion passed through me from behind and out the other side like radio waves. *If you've got too much to hold on to, let go.*

The girl I loved had tried to kill me, and I forgave her before the flames died, and the smoke finished rising over the forest, watching from the safety of wet trees.

After all, she had run out of words.

They found her remains in the kitchen, from where the fire had spread, holding in one decimated hand an indestructible key. It was identified by its teeth as belonging to the back door.

One year later, the section of Summer House ravaged by flames had been rebuilt. The kitchen had gone along with my bedroom above, but my father's study and the rest of the house remained intact. There was the heavy rain to thank, and the firemen pointed to the rock-solid infrastructure. New rooms completed a replica of the building as it had stood before.

I spoke to my father, who had indeed been asked by Imogen to leave me alone. I did not ask him why he had followed this directive, but told him that he had done me a kind of favour, and that I would tell him the whole story some day.

When Jenny was in London, I tried to get in touch. I didn't see much of Jonny. I began to call up some old friends. The world seemed more tangible now, like I was facing, but slowly dismantling, a brick wall. Like an old acquaintance, familiar but changed, the future began to re-emerge.

I went back to Summer House a number of times in the following months, once the rebuilding work was completed, each time by myself, to continue a kind of vigil.

I thought about Imogen a lot, of the way in which she had chosen to add to my loss.

One morning, I was looking for a novel in my suitcase. I found myself staring at a black notebook, the drive of my thoughts stalled.

It seemed charged with an impetus of its own. Did I buy it, use it? It had been there for months, I was sure.

The first page was dated simply '1989'.

How to begin?

Imogen's journal.

Had she given it to me? I could not recall this having happened. She had left it at my flat by accident then, I had scooped it up amongst the other books I packed. Perhaps she left it there on purpose. I turned the journal over in my hands, pictured her sliding it under the books on my coffee table, sensing the time we spent together was coming to an end.

I took it to my father's study, retrieved the Midnightsong papers from his filing cabinet, handwritten on faint-lined paper, kept in a brown card envelope. Placed them next to the journal on the desk. And I remembered how Imogen Taylor had arrived at my flat, keen to have me understand how important the contents of her journal would prove to be for me. She had experienced an overwhelming feeling of anticipation, when she reread the parts of it that recorded her following my mother through Belsize Park and beyond, before she met me. She said that, eventually, we might swap these two books, in a ceremony of binding trust suggested audaciously at the outset.

Placing one palm on top of the journal, the other on Midnightsong, I slid them around one other, crossing my arms.

And gave myself permission to read.

Imogen's handwriting was small and of exquisite consistency, running to the edge of each unruled page. I scanned the first half of the book – the second was blank – till I caught my mother's name, then her initial, repeated a number of times on the same page. This particular entry was dated June 17th, '92. Wherever I was in the world she was writing of, I would have been nine years old. Imogen would have been about fifteen.

Among the long paragraphs were the following sentences:

M. enters supermarket. Comes out with two shopping bags.

M. walks slowly past Belsize Park Tube. Looking at the sky?

M. wanders into small playground on Primrose Hill, comes out again.

M. in café, drinking coffee, reading paper.

M. standing next to shop, smoking cigarette!!!

I had seen my mother smoke the occasional cigarette when I was a child, so despite the string of exclamation marks, I found this revelation unremarkable. Clearly, the simple thrill of following her had intoxicated Imogen.

The final line for this entry read:

Returns to the house, lets herself in, shutting door.

I continued to read.

June 18th, '92

Mum bought me the wrong shoes yesterday. She looked so pleased when I put them on – and she paid for them – I couldn't say anything. I thought I'd take them back and change them after school today, pretend they hurt and the other colour was the only one left. Well, I still had to wear them into school, because Mum dropped me off. Someone was shouting straightaway, and Mum stayed by the gate for a while which made it worse. I just kept walking, I hope she didn't hear (the shoes are like black trainers with thick, curvy soles).

I went and sat in the toilets before registration. It was too late to borrow someone else's, too many people had seen me already. I thought about pretending to faint, but how silly would I look, spread out across the classroom floor in those shoes! I told myself that no one else would notice, that the worst was over. Well, I got upset, and stayed where I was, sitting on the lid of the toilet, with the cubicle door locked. Jessica Chapman came in, I heard her humming to herself. She started banging on the door. I stayed quiet. Oh, it's you, she said. She left, and didn't mention the shoes (she doesn't care about that, Imogen!). When everything went quiet again, I knelt on the floor and got on with it. Afterwards felt dizzy.

I stopped reading, horrified.
Got on with what? Was she throwing up? Cutting herself?
I flicked forwards.
One entry glittered among the rest like a carefully cut jewel, written when she was eighteen.

The shore was littered with shells, and the sea was blue. There was a breeze in the mornings. I'd go there when it was barely light. Then the sea was dark too. This will sound silly, but I thought it was like the future. You can only go so far out when you get in. You have to stay near the shore. But it's all just out there, the currents, the quiet.

It's like nostalgia for home. You want to reach out and take hold of the distance, make it your own. Be free from here and now, today and tomorrow. But you can't, and so you try to be patient, make do with looking and thinking. With what you can see in front of you. You have to make do.

If I'm looking at the sea, I don't know. I guess it brings me closer to everybody else who's seen it, at that time, by themselves. We've all lost something behind the horizon. Maybe we don't know what it is. We're all together when we're alone.

The Sighting

'Time's up,' said Jonny.

We were sitting under a tree that stood at the end of the garden, protecting it from the weight of the afternoon sunlight. The smoke from my cigarette traced the minute fluctuations in the air overhead, whorled across the shadows in the leaves. The leaves broke up the sky, so that, leaning back in my chair, I could let my hair fall, narrow my eyes, see glints of light like stars gliding above me.

I could see my brother in my peripheral vision, sense him looking at me.

'Full costume. Marie Antoinette. Big hair. Big dress. Impractical.'

'Seriously,' I said.

His champagne glass gleamed in the corner of my eye.

'Blue dress. It has to be. She's only got one left.'

A blue blur moved out from behind him. Jenny was walking from the villa towards us. She smiled as she approached. The outline of Fiesole Hill swept up behind her right shoulder. Other, grander houses were distributed across the green slope, visible in shards and sections. She passed over the view of Florence.

'Something funny?' said Jenny, sitting down.

She took a cigarette from my pack and lit it.

'Those things aren't free, you know,' I said.

'They are in Italy.'

'We weren't laughing at you,' said Jonny.

'It's too hot to laugh,' said Jenny.

'It's too hot to think. I might go to sleep,' I said.

She turned to me.

'The taxi's here in half an hour.'

'Remind me what we're doing this afternoon?'

'Shopping.'

I let my head fall back again, relaxed my arms. Maybe I would let Jenny take charge today. She had been formidable since we arrived, and I could feel a kind of numbness developing inside me, making my body heavy and my mind airy, apathetic. Besides, shopping was Jenny's area of expertise. She already had a list of boutiques we would go and see.

The party for the seventh anniversary of my mother's death was to be held the following evening. My father had hired a second villa in the south of the city, where the roads wound into the trees and hills beyond the Oltrarno. Fifty guests had come from England and elsewhere, mainly family, Marianne's agent and her American agent, a few friends she had managed to keep, some she had lost contact with. A friend of Jonny's. They were down there somewhere, wandering the city, some staying in hotels, others in the hired villa itself. We had decided that we wanted to stay up on the hill, but the impossibility of returning to the old place had gone without question.

'Shopping with Jenny. What to wear? I guess I'll have to make an effort,' I said.

Jenny frowned.

'Damn right, you will.'

We left the taxi on the Via de Tornabuoni. Jenny gravitated towards the window of Hermés. Bright silk handkerchiefs were flung across a black chaise-longue, the gold rims of cups and saucers rippled round mannequins and props.

'The only way you're getting something here is if I go to the party in jeans,' I said. 'How much has Dad given us?'

'Not enough,' said Jenny, walking past me towards the Duomo.

I followed a little behind, sidestepping the crowds.

'What colour are you going for?' I said.

'Something light. Maybe white. You?'

'Black. I won't get bored of it. I can wear it again.'

'There's nothing wrong with wearing something once.'

'I don't think Mum would have wanted us to go out of our way.'

We stopped in front of another window. It contained a white dress. Jenny stooped to examine it.

'It's probably her money,' I said.

'Buying a dress is supposed to be a straightforward process.'

'I'll hold you to that. After you.'

The door was opened for us.

'I'm not sure black is appropriate, either,' she continued. 'We said it was going to be a celebration.'

'For me, that means not thinking about the colour. Relaxing, not trying too hard.'

'We should avoid the funeral effect.'

'I'm enjoying myself already.'

Jenny pulled the corner of the skirt of a dress. It opened from the railing like a fan.

'I'm glad you're looking forward to it,' she said.

She took it to the changing rooms. I followed.

'Why are we doing it?' she said from behind the curtain.

'It's about remembering her. Talking about her to the people there. Finding a sense of peace about the whole thing. Each being our own person. Growing up. That kind of thing.'

Jenny was quiet for a few minutes. I pulled the curtain back. She was sitting in the new dress, its voluminous skirt crushed under her. She had been crying. I dropped to her eye-level, put a hand on her shoulder.

'What's wrong?'

She shook her head.

'Don't worry. We can sit here for a while,' I said.

I tried to see things from her perspective. Jenny had been tightly wound since we arrived, changing clothes twice a day, going down to the villa where the party was to take place, obsessing over the aesthetics of the event. She had looked forward to this shopping trip.

'Hey. Say something to me.'

'This is the one. It's very expensive.'

Outside, I gave her a hug and hailed a cab. She climbed, dwarfed by her enormous shopping bag. I waved her off, headed for the Uffizi. I knew the house would be too quiet for me that evening. A surplus of time that would stealthily enervate us all. I passed the queues, bought a ticket at the booking office, sat on the wall above the Arno to wait. The green water moved slowly below the hectic streets. I willed the sunlight, which sharpened the edges of the buildings around me, to infuse my skin, dry out the channels of adrenaline that would sparkle momentarily, receding with their glint of danger.

Inside, I climbed the stairs, slipped into a space before La Primavera. The painting looked blanched, too pale compared to the reproduction I had learnt in the book I had at home. But the strange tableau was surrounded by the orange trees I did remember, and here the vividness of the fruit set against the shards of blue sky gave me the pleasure I had hoped for and predicted.

Next, I headed for the galleries of the Palazzo Pitti, saw Raphael's Madonna and Child with St. John the Baptist, decked in harlequin colours, and Titian's Mary Magdalene, its voluptuous subject gazing beyond the picture's frame, wrapped in the fertile flow of her own hair. Walking into the dense air of the Boboli Gardens, up the hill by interchanging pathways, I felt giddy, as though I was drifting on the intermittent breezes, my mind expanding to cover the sloping grounds around me. What struck me when I turned in a small, annexed garden I had wandered through, to see the city silenced and smoothed out beneath me, were the colours on offer, colours I could recognise from the museums below.

This I can do, I thought. I resolved to study Art History at university. This I can do and be me.

I enjoyed the way in which I made the city a metaphor then, for the quiet expanse of my undiscovered future, countless streets working in every direction, turning around the unseen villa with the white marquee where, tomorrow, I would alight.

'I'd like to arrive as a guest would. By myself,' I had said the previous night.

'Not many guests would arrive by themselves,' said Dad.

'I want to see everything from the outside.'

'Whatever makes you happy.'

I stepped out of the taxi alone.

The path that led round the side of the villa was hazy with evening shadows. The pungency of wilting flowers thickened the air. Through a break in the trees, I glimpsed a cluster of white fairy lights. Stopped where I stood. A breeze was pushing against my back. Shut my eyes.

Imagined that my mother was at the party. That we would not meet, but that she had found her way there.

I stood for a moment longer under the blackening sky.

In the garden, I saw Dad immediately, sitting at a table with Julia Preston, formerly my mother's agent, and some people I did not recognise. He was laughing, the sound lost in the clamour of the crowd.

Julia vanished, reappeared beside me, gave me a hug.

'How wonderful this is,' she said. 'Your old man is surprisingly adept at throwing parties. Although I only saw him once it started to get dark. I'm still not convinced that he emerges in the daytime.'

'He's been here since three, believe it or not. Sorting things. I should go over.'

'Your brother and sister are looking for you. But I saw you and I wanted to say hello. Your mother would have been so proud of you. You look wonderful.'

'Thank you.'

'Now, off you go.'

She returned to the table.

The crowd made way for me, familiar faces smiling, occasionally leaning in to make conversation. I stopped by the bar, narrowed my eyes against the noise and watched the passing wine glasses conducting light, the stop-start glimmer of jewellery, an incandescent stream meandering through the night air, in and out of the marquee. Jonny and Jenny, I thought. Tonight is about people, not silent reveries. I knew who I was, and why I was here. Circling the tent, I found them at the back with Jonny's friend, sitting at a stolen table.

Jenny pushed a bottle of vodka towards me.

'You need to catch up.'

'It's like that, is it?' I said.

Jonny's friend grinned.

'It took me a long time to get here,' he said. 'I was promised proper drinking.'

'This is Steve,' said Jonny. 'He's run out of conversation already.'

'Well, I'm an awkward person,' said Steve. 'Vodka helps.'

Jenny was looking at me. There were three empty champagne flutes on the table, three empty shot glasses.

'Already?' I said.

My brother and sister didn't reply. Steve grunted again.

'Don't mind these two,' he said. 'They've been like this all night.'

'You sound surprised,' I said.

Steve held up his hands.

'Just helping you catch up.'

I poured myself a shot.

'What about all those people?' I said. 'Half the faces I recognise, but can't place.'

'You added a real buzz,' said Jenny. 'In particular.'

'How so?' I said.

'Everybody's staring at you.'

'Nice of you to say so.'

'Why could that be?'

'Drop it, Jenny,' said my brother.

'You came dressed as Mum. Maybe that's it.'

I looked at Steve.

'Did you see Dad's face?' she said. 'When you arrived?'

'I can't help it if there's a resemblance.'

'You're dressed like her. You have your hair the same way. Of course you don't mind. You live in your own head, after all.'

'What is this?' I said.

I turned to Jonny. He looked at the table.

'You're wearing Mum's pearls,' said Jenny.

'That's right,' I said.

'That's right!' Jenny shouted. She stood up, knocking her chair over backwards.

'If I look like her, it's an accident.'

'It's one way to get attention, isn't it?'

'I came here to celebrate her life.'

I was shaking.

Jenny walked away. I looked at Jonny. He watched Jenny leave, stood up.

'We need to let Dad know.'

I followed him.

My father led us to the side of the house. They stood away from me, began to argue.

'You worked on this all afternoon,' said Dad.

'You're either drunk or delusional.'

'You can still redeem yourself. Go and bring your sister back. Before she gets lost.'

'I'm sorry,' I said. 'It's my fault.'

They looked away.

I walked to the main road, headed for the city. The ground beneath me seemed unsteady. I bent to take my heels off. It was not the alcohol, which strengthened the glow of the street lights, energising me now. It was the feeling from the day before, of my muscles becoming slow and heavy, turned as easily from a sensation of peace to one of dread, as a river flows and adjusts itself to an imperceptible bend.

Jenny was sitting beneath a street lamp, on the wall of the embankment. I stopped some distance away, held my breath. She stood up, began to walk along the wall between the lit road and the hidden drop.

Her back was straight, heels clacking slowly, testing the stone surface.

I did not want to shout, to surprise her. I pictured her falling to the walkway on the blind side, every bone in her body shattering.

Get down.

I lay my shoes on the pavement soundlessly. Crept up behind. Pulled her towards me.

It seemed as though she lived her own death. She screamed before we hit the pavement, then she began to cry, unstoppable.

'You came for me,' she said.

I understood what she meant. Saw her knocking on the downstairs window of our house in Belsize Park. I addressed what I knew I could.

'I didn't realise what I looked like. It's the truth.'

'It would be too weird if you did.'

'Sometimes I don't know how to get things out.'

'You're doing fine.'

We sat in silence for a while.

'Funny,' I said. 'I wondered if she would be here tonight.'

'I'm glad she wasn't,' said Jenny. 'I might have said the wrong thing.'

We were sitting with our backs to the wall. Jenny was staring at the kerb, her chin on her knees, arms wrapped round her shins.

'You gave me a fright,' I said.

'Got you back.'

A car pulled up. Dad was driving, Jonny was in the passenger seat. We got to our feet and climbed in. We passed along the river, through a sudden crowd at the edge of the Ponte Vecchio, before the old city faded, roundabouts and billboards appeared, then we were heading up, the lights of the hillside falling on our right, villas drifting down towards the town like paper lanterns.

I closed my eyes. Stars sliding.

'Look at that,' said Jonny.

My father pulled the car into a lay-by. I sat up.

'Look at what?'

Jenny blinked at me, uncomprehendingly. She had been asleep.

We left the car, stood at the edge of the road, looked up the hill which tilted away into the night. In the distance, a flare of yellow and white probed the darkness.

'Fire,' said Jenny.

There were sparks, a brief streak of red.

'I'm not sure we should be watching this,' I said.

'Let's go up there,' said Jonny.

My father cleared his throat.

'It's probably just a bonfire. But on this trip I wanted to tell you what happened that night. Maybe now's a good time.'

For a while nobody spoke.

'Your mother had been in fantastic spirits that day. We were talking about secondary schools for Isabel, having discussed the matter in code for weeks. Your mother was excited, we quickly came to a decision. Imagining you in navy blue, at sports day and so on. As was so often the case, the discussion made formal what we had already worked out tacitly. We had even left a navy jumper out for you to wear, to get used to, which we could see you liked. Underhand tactics. You liked that it was the same colour as your brother's. Well, we looked around us. Surveyed the scene. Jenny was reading her first proper novel upstairs. And Jonny had solved a dispute between your mother and her agent that took place a couple of days before. Marianne was explaining the problem to me in the kitchen. I can't remember what it was about. But you passed through and told her casually what she should do. And she was open-mouthed. So we decided after you'd gone that somebody who spoke like that could easily handle the babysitting. As could Isabel, of course. Childminding, sorry. I always asked your mother to put it like that.' He scratched his cheek. 'We left for the party, the world laid out before us, not without a mutual feeling of self-congratulation. When we arrived, your mother was immediately cornered by a horrendous creature, I can't remember her name. But I watched Annie from across the room. The woman who had approached her was talking loudly about an article she was writing, twenty ways to ensnare the man of your dreams, that kind of thing. Don't get crumbs around your mouth on dates. Therefore, don't eat if possible. Even better, don't show up. I saw your mother reach up to her ears once or twice. At first I thought she was fidgeting, bored out of her mind, then I realised what she had realised. She had forgotten to wear the diamond earrings I gave her for our anniversary, recently passed. I'm afraid we enjoyed concealing this date from you. Don't ask me why. Your mother came over shortly and told me she was heading home. That she would be fifteen minutes, max. I looked at the tiny dimple on her left ear lobe as she spoke to me, tried to decide if I preferred it with jewellery or not. I think she knew what I was thinking about, because she insisted on going. Then I remember being trapped by that woman, sounding her theories out to me. One of the worst experiences at a drinks party I believe I've ever had.' He laughed. 'Then I remember driving. Which brings us up to date.'

Jonny was fixed on the fire.

I turned to Jenny.

She was scratching her head.

Sitting up late in the sitting room at Summer House one night, I thought about my mother's books. At some point, each of her protagonists is mystified by a supply of courage that is granted them, enabling them to step across boundaries in their lives, previously unseen. Joseph Long leaves his family, is prepared to question his sanity in Thunder, Lightning. Sarah Morgan reimagines the bullying that blighted her childhood in The Black Cloche. Celine Curtis feels she is out of her depth socially, at the French château in Naked Light and, perhaps, ends up committing suicide. The consequences of pushing forwards are sometimes terrifying. But as each understands the limits of his or her life, each recognises that they have no choice. Perhaps they change without realising.

It was winter again. I watched the light that fell from the windows onto the lawn outside, pushing the night back into the near distance. A fox ran across the lit part of the garden, leaving small depressions in the frosted grass. I began to think of the part that light played in my mother's work. Suffocating heat, a finger of lightning, a dream's panic room filled with candle flame. Light continually lifts the curtain on the world, opening up new terrain.

That evening, before I made for my father's study to fetch Midnightsong, I ran through the following scene in my head, one that takes place near the end of The Black Cloche:

Mrs. Morgan opened her eyes, moaned softly, felt her body for bruises, remembered where she was. The room was filled with twilight. As she tried to remember what combination of doors and corridors had led her there, her daughter's face flashed in her mind. She stood unsteadily. The man with the smooth, pale face smiled at the door. He took her hand, led her down a spiralling flight of steps, holding a candle before them. A corona settled around his head, the stone wall quivered as it unwound.

B.C.

MIDNIGHTSONG

Fragment 1

The first fragment contains the first few pages of the novel. Count Putti, master of the Palazzo Crescentini, is preparing for a trip to Florence, where he will present his new bride to Lorenzo de' Medici. The night before his departure, he imagines his wife, Sofia, somewhere beneath him in the depths of the building, singing and combing her blonde hair. He sees her in his mind's eye from above, feels a rising sense of dread.

> The lustre of her hair blurred and drifted as though he saw her underwater, and he was passing over the surface, beating heavy wings.

As he pictures 'each bright strand of hair pulled taut', he looks out of the window, over the forest, towards the misted hills of Florence, and understands that there is something he is refusing to admit to himself.

Fragment 2

Putti is running through a series of possibilities in his mind: methods of leaving a building. He pictures Sofia passing between the doors of a murky cellar, lowering herself from a window on a rope of rags tied end-to-end,

> stepping out of various exits into the evening, her hairpin catching on the moonlight.

Fragment 3

A girl with blonde hair is in his private quarters. He has not seen her before and he confronts her. She explains that she is new to the house, has wandered into these rooms by mistake. Her voice is toneless, unaccented. She lets a comb of his that she has palmed slip from her hand back onto the dressing table. Later, he discovers long, curling threads of gold wrapped round its tines.

The sun comes up and the count decides that he will stay in the palace for one more week.

Fragment 4

Sofia is shivering, riding into the forest that sweeps out beneath the palace, on horseback. A group of men are riding behind her, carrying tapers. The Count is among them. It is night-time. Something has happened. She does not try to turn round, to catch his eye. One of the men pulls his horse into step alongside hers, says something to her quietly. She tugs on the reins, dismounts. And waits. Something understood by all present is considered by all, for a moment, in silence. Then the same man waves her away with his sword. She disappears into the trees.

Fragment 5

She is running, breathless, fearful.

Her dress seemed to shred instantly on contact with the branches that the darkness produced like dead bouquets from a velvet hat.

Gradually, time dissipated, rippling outwards from her footsteps'
fall, and soon she felt propelled forwards by the same hushed energy
that made the trees grow, the stars turn to diamond in the black
crush of night.

Fragment 6

Sofia finds a small river and follows it downstream. A bridge
appears in the distance, 'traced by pinpoint lights on the
surface of the night'. She makes her way towards it, eating tiny
berries that she knows are harmless. Perhaps she has been in
the forest for more than one night.

As she approaches the bridge, it swings about, turns into a
boat laden with candlelight. A woman with jewels in her hair
who reminds her of somebody stands at the stern holding an oar,
ushers her in, and silently they are released to the water's current.
'The light-brushed forest rearranged itself around them.' As
they round a curve in the river, a small church emerges from
the foliage, apparently underlit, pale against the night sky.

Another appeared, sallying towards them, then another, before
the Duomo itself rose out of the trees, adrift like a strange ark on
the surface of the trees.

Sofia's hands are static in her lap. If she fears she might be
mad, she does not show it.

When the boat draws into the river bank again, Sofia climbs
out. She walks back into the forest. The trees are widely spaced
here, soft grass grows between the trunks like a great carpet,
silver in the bright moonlight.

She passed an orange tree, blooming anomalously beneath a
patch of open sky. Instead of fruit, glass spheres hung from its

black branches, each appearing to contain a miniature forest, baubles that she might have strung across the wall over the palace staircase, around the frame of her four-poster bed.

Fragment 7

Dogs bark in the distance. She climbs a tall tree, stretches out across the strongest bough, waits for the noise to disappear. She hums to herself.

Fragment 8

Sofia emerges into a clearing, into the full glare of the moonlight.

Dark objects were dispersed across the flat grass. She reached out, felt the cool grain of her ebony chest-of-drawers, opened her wardrobe, touched the fabrics hanging in shadow inside. Her bed was a shut box, the curtains drawn. The apparatus of her dressing table sparkled beneath its shuttered mirror.

She moved on, to a path that opened into a second clearing.

Two chairs are set by a long table, heavily laden with food, which is warm. She sits until dawn arrives and the sky turns pink, orange, into streaks of faint green.

The banquet set before her coloured and fructified, crimson hams and buttered potatoes forming, promising to dissolve again on the tongue. A large jug of milk stood next to her arm, a flotilla of bubbles marking the surface. Oranges were piled on a white bowl. Two glasses filled with vermilion wine. When she heard the dogs barking again, Sofia decided that this time she would not run away.

After finishing, I found a pen and paper, and tried to fill in the gaps.

If we want to try to make sense of the fragments, we have to begin with the question of who Count Putti's wife is, and why, at the start, he is exploring the ways in which she could escape from the palace. Either he is playing a game with himself, or he fears that her leaving him in secret is a real possibility. His attempts to picture her suggest a desire to hold and to examine her in his mind. His attention to extreme detail suggests the pressure of paranoia.

A blonde woman appears in one of his own rooms. The comb she lets slip from her hand must be his. But who is she? She may be a stranger, who disturbs him by the resemblance she bears to his wife. There is something ghostlike about her, her unaccented voice, something unfixable. She is an intruder, relinquishing the comb like a stolen object. Perhaps she is a maid, newly acquired, who has been caught exploring, prying where she should not, made ethereal by her sudden entrapment in the Count's paranoid web of association. He fears that his wife wants to find a way out of their marriage. Perhaps she is a spirit of his own mind, a version of Sofia, visiting his rooms to take a souvenir of an ill-fated union. Seized by fear, she lets the comb slip from her hand.

Alternatively, we could be in the midst of a flashback. Perhaps this is actually his first meeting with his wife, a year or two before. Sofia has dared to creep into his chambers. She is surprised there, unfamiliar with her surroundings.

We do not know what he thinks and feels upon seeing her. But we can sense, already, that this is a world which is circumscribed by Putti's mind.

Then follows the part in which Sofia is followed into the forest by Putti and the men on horseback, carrying flaming torches. Here there are three strong possibilities. Perhaps she is being banished, driven out by her husband, who has been overpowered now by his fears of her imminent escape. This interpretation seems to collapse when later events are considered. Given what Sofia will now experience, as she wanders, runs through the forest, it does not seem as though she has seen the last of this trickster.

Perhaps, then, she is entering into a kind of game, willingly or unwillingly. A number of obstacles have been set up for her to make her way past.

This would make the count an illusionist of some kind, providing his wife with an adventure of the senses. He has devised a phantasmagoric journey that she will undertake. He is cast as a man of leisure with a vast imagination. The theory begins to falter when Sofia hears dogs barking behind her. She spends much of her journey running, gasping for oxygen. When she climbs the tree, she is not playing hide-and-seek.

The third, and most likely, possibility, is that a combination of the two scenarios is taking place. Putti has invented an adventure for Sofia. But it is an adventure designed to punish her. It is a kind of exile. It is a test of some kind, a means by which to teach Sofia something. Her participation is compulsory.

It would be natural to assume, since their relationship is central to the story, that an infidelity has taken place, or is perceived to have taken place, on Sofia's part. What follows is Putti's response. However, an infidelity in the obvious sense is not so much as hinted at in the fragments. Therefore, let us assume that Sofia has committed a more subtle form of infidelity. She has neglected the count, or failed to become for him the dependent wife that he imagined. His early attempt to picture her suggests that he finds her remote, separate, difficult to comprehend. He devises an experience for her, that will enable him to understand what she is made of, that will imprint his authority indelibly upon her mind. She is to be forced beyond herself, in order to know him better. There will be a life's worth of emotion and sensory bombardment, compressed into a single night, into the opening and closing of an eye. The hunter and the hunted will be united by an experience that will mark them both for life.

In the forest, she is lost in a shadow-world, made to run from a fear at first unquantifiable. She must survive by her own initiative: eating berries, drinking from streams. At the river, the burning bridge becomes a boat, a dead end transforms into a way forwards. She must accept help from a stranger, who is played, perhaps, by a half-remembered figure from the palace retinue. Bloodied and exhausted, Sofia finally reaches a passive state in the vessel, helpless to do anything other than rest. Then she is shown giant, ghostly churches, that rise up inexplicably at the water's edge.

Perhaps we are meant to assume they are wooden façades, that the count has had constructed and lit up. Perhaps there is something more mysterious going on. Either way, Sofia seems to see bewitching apparitions. The outside world is creeping into the shadow-forest, dismantled and distorted, as in a dream.

She disembarks, moves through changing terrain, finds a tree that holds impossible fruit. In the black mirror of each sphere, Sofia observes the world reflected, many times over. Next she finds her private possessions, her toilet and furniture strewn across a clearing, her bedchamber relocated to the forest floor.

We are supposed to sense a calm coming over her, a growing understanding of what has happened. She has seen the world transformed into a picture lantern, come to know the condensed rhythms of the river and the woods. Finally, in the tree's crystal appendages, she has seen an image of the conscious mind, reflective and anomalous against the backdrop of sleeping nature. In the moonlit clearing, the reader must race to catch up with her. She has flown from death and found her way home, to the touch of carved and chamfered wood, the woven material behind the wardrobe door.

And what next? Who is about to join her at the supper table, laid out at breakfast time, just as the sun is rising?

Of course, it must be Putti.

He will sit across from her in silence, wait to hear what she has made of her voyage. And she will sit in silence, also, waiting for the sunlight to strengthen and show her the exact expression on his face. The hounds will lope out from the trees, rest their jaws on their forelegs and wait for strips of fat and bone to be passed down to them. When the tablecloth turns to gleaming snow, and the silverware burns with white light, the couple will finally turn to face each other.

I finished writing, wondered what Imogen would have made of it.

Trying to picture the dark forest floor, I remembered a story my mother had told, in one of the few interviews she had granted. She spoke of a dream she had had, of the floor giving way beneath her bed, waking whilst falling. The nightmare everyone's experienced, familiar as we all are with creaking floors, a fear of holes, of the dark, of that which is solid dissolving.

In the garden at the villa in Florence, she had stepped out over darkness, recreated the drop into black. Awake, when there is often a limit to the things of the world, a finite width and depth.

If Sofia wants to escape from her palace in Midnightsong, Putti wants to direct that escape back to himself. Her outward journey forms a circle. I decided that my mother felt an urge to escape from her own palace also. That she found domestic family life impossible, longed to slip off into unmapped landscapes. She journeyed through her stories to distant places in her mind, only to find herself back where she started. She must have envisioned many other exits, I decided, before she chose the most terrifying. Like divorcing Dad, buying a new house elsewhere. In another city, another country.

Maybe Imogen had just wanted to protect me. To take the blame from my Mum for killing herself by fire that night in our family home. Maybe Imogen knew what she did and didn't want to believe it. Maybe she loved Marianne Sykes more than me.

Did she want a different family?

Did she want to be by herself?

The questions could have referred to Marianne or Imogen.

Had she loved me?

One thing I learned from each of them: the dead are not equations to be solved, any more than the waking.